deep green

D0204407

deep green

color me jealous

melody carlson

NAVPRESS

Discipleship Inside Out™

THINK

NAVPRESS
Discipleship Inside Out™

NavPress is the publishing ministry of The Navigators, an international Christian organization and leader in personal spiritual development. NavPress is committed to helping people grow spiritually and enjoy lives of meaning and hope through personal and group resources that are biblically rooted, culturally relevant, and highly practical.

**For a free catalog go to www.NavPress.com
or call 1.800.366.7788 in the United States or 1.800.839.4769 in Canada.**

ISBN 13: 978-157683-530-2

Cover design by David Carlson Design
Cover photo by Alamy Images
Creative Team: Jay Howver, Erin Healy, Cara Iverson, Glynese Northam

This is a work of fiction. The characters, incidents, and dialogues are products of the author's imagination and are not to be construed as real. Any resemblance to actual events or persons, living or dead, is entirely coincidental.

Published in association with the literary agency of Sara A. Fortenberry.

Carlson, Melody.
  Deep green : color me jealous / Melody Carlson.
      p. cm. -- (TrueColors ; bk. 2)
  Summary: A Christian high school girl considers having sex with a former boyfriend in order to win him back.
  ISBN 1-57683-530-8
  [1. Jealousy--Fiction. 2. Dating (Social customs)--Fiction. 3. Christian life--Fiction.]
  I. Title.
  PZ7.C216637Dee 2004
  [Fic]--dc22
                                2004000282

Printed in the United States of America

7 8 9 10 11 12 / 15 14 13 12 11

Other Books by Melody Carlson

Harsh Pink (NavPress)

Moon White (NavPress)

Bright Purple (NavPress)

Faded Denim (NavPress)

Bitter Rose (NavPress)

Blade Silver (NavPress)

Fool's Gold (NavPress)

Burnt Orange (NavPress)

Pitch Black (NavPress)

Torch Red (NavPress)

Dark Blue (NavPress)

DIARY OF A TEENAGE GIRL series (Multnomah)

DEGREES series (Tyndale)

Crystal Lies (WaterBrook)

Finding Alice (WaterBrook)

Three Days (Baker)

On This Day (WaterBrook)

one

I KNOW WHAT EVERYONE'S BEEN SAYING ABOUT ME, BUT HONESTLY IT'S NOT my fault that Timothy Lawrence dumped Shawna Frye the day after the Harvest Dance. Really, it's just the way life happened. I mean, just because you've gone with a guy for a year doesn't mean you *own* him. Besides, I didn't see any engagement ring on Shawna's finger. She swears Timothy got her a promise ring last summer that she lost swimming at the lake. Yeah, right. It's not like Shawna is the most honest person on the planet. I mean, she's been saying all kinds of crud about me lately. And not only are they total figments of her imagination but they're totally mean too.

I overheard her talking to Lucy Farrell in the locker room today. "Jordan Ferguson is a backstabbing tramp," she said in this cruel voice that didn't even sound like her. Of course, Shawna didn't realize that I could hear her going on and on from behind the closed door of the bathroom stall. Or maybe she did. Maybe she just didn't care that her words cut me deeply. But everyone knows she's out to get me. It's what's driving her these days. I'm just glad she's not the violent type (at least I don't think she is). Just the same, I've been watching my back, and I wouldn't be surprised if she pulled some weird kind of vengeful stunt, like letting her side of the pyramid collapse while I am precariously balanced on top. Of course, I always have to be on top since I'm the smallest cheerleader—just one more reason why I need to get this stupid mess sorted out ASAP.

So, while I was holed up in the bathroom stall, no pun intended, I had to ask myself why on earth Shawna was telling all this to Lucy Farrell. I mean, Lucy's nice enough, but she's not exactly that involved in our group of friends, and frankly it's none of her business. But I suspect Shawna's just looking for new sets of ears since everyone else is probably sick and tired of hearing her whine and complain about me all the time.

The really sad part in all this is that I honestly thought Shawna and I were friends. *Good* friends even. And I really liked her. Next to my old best friend, Kara Hendricks, Shawna was the best friend I'd ever had. She's fun and funny, and we're both cheerleaders, and we like the same kinds of things (including the same boys, as it turns out), but I'd really hoped we could be friends for a long, long time.

"Didn't you think she'd get mad when you stole her boyfriend?" Amber Elliot asked me the other day. It didn't help that Amber was staring at me like I was the village idiot. Like, *Duh, how dumb are you, Jordan Ferguson?*

But the truth is I really didn't think Shawna would care that much. "I told you that Timothy said they were *over with*," I explained to Amber in my most convincing tone. "He *said* that they both knew their relationship was *history* and that they were only staying together through the Harvest Dance and only because he'd promised to take her."

"That's not what Shawna says." Amber was giving me her no-nonsense look. Now, Amber's African-American and the kind of girl who doesn't put up with anything. I suppose that's one reason she makes such a good head cheerleader. Well, that and she's just really good at it, not to mention incredibly gorgeous. Think Halle Berry kind of gorgeous. I mean, this girl really turns heads.

But back to me, which I know sounds a bit narcissistic, but the honest truth is, I'm not as much self-centered as I am a bit obsessive-compulsive. Just ask my friend Kara. And I'm trying to deal with it. But that's another problem altogether.

Still, the really hard part about all this latest brouhaha (I used that word in speech once and it means something like "much ado about nothing") is that I'm the new girl in this particular group. See, I only became a cheerleader this fall, and it still feels like I have to prove myself on pretty much a daily basis. And it doesn't help that everyone else in this group is pretty loyal to Shawna, who's been in this group for years now. Anyway, most of them have sided with her already.

Amber's about the only one who's tried to keep the middle ground, but that might have more to do with being head cheerleader than with being my friend. Still, I haven't given up on her alliance.

"What do you think I should do?" I asked her today. "Should I break up with Timothy?" Of course, I knew that no matter what she said I probably wouldn't do this. I don't even know if I *could* do this—that's how much I like this guy. But I was curious about what she'd say.

"I'm not about to go there," she said, "but you and Shawna better sort this thing out before basketball season starts. We can't have two snarling cheerleaders spoiling the morale for everyone else."

I forced my best smile. "I'm trying, Amber, really I am. But Shawna won't even speak to me."

"Well, give her time to chill." Amber rolled her big brown eyes dramatically. "Thank goodness football season is almost over with."

"Tim says basketball season is supposed to be really good," I said, hoping to encourage her.

"Yeah, it's *supposed* to be. Let's just hope the cheerleaders can do their part to keep it together without someone getting murdered before the season is over." She looked at me like I was personally responsible for the morale of the entire team. "I gotta go now."

I waved goodbye and wished I had said something more convincing. I mean, I could really use someone like Amber to be solidly on my side. The truth is, I feel pretty alone right now. Even Kara Hendricks, my old best friend, seems to be holding me at arm's length these days. But at least I have my Timothy. Now, *that's* some consolation prize!

I can't deny that I've had the hots for Tim ever since last year. He was a junior then but already playing on the varsity basketball team, he's that good. And speaking of good, he's not bad-looking either. Ha! He's actually so good-looking that, according to Shawna, a local modeling agency approached him about being in some ads, but he turned them down, which I think is a shame because I'm willing to bet he's very photogenic with those big dark brown eyes and his naturally blond hair. Not to mention that he always looks tan. He says it's his Native American blood, but I wonder if he doesn't sneak off to the tanning booths occasionally.

Of course, Timothy didn't have a clue last year that I was infatuated with him. Mostly he didn't even know that I existed, since I was still pretty much a nobody. Plus he was going with Shawna, one of the coolest girls in the school. Just the same, I enjoyed watching Timothy from a distance. And I used to cheer for him from the bleachers like he was the only one down there—or on the planet for that matter. I suppose I was obsessing a little. But believe me, he looked totally awesome in that blue and red uniform. I loved watching him dribble the ball down the court with such smooth confidence. Most of all, I liked his smile. I still do.

Of course, I *never* told a single person any of this. It was like my clandestine obsession. I didn't even tell Kara, and we were still pretty close at the time. I guess my feeling is that when you really, really like someone, it's best to play your cards close to your chest (as my dad would say). It gives you the advantage. And I think that has a lot to do with how I finally managed to hook Timothy. Whenever I was hanging with my new circle of friends and Timothy was around, I would just act all nonchalant and laid back, like *I could take you or leave you, Timothy Lawrence.* Sure, I'd laugh at his jokes—he's a real teaser too—but then I'd just toss it right back at him as if I didn't even care what he thought about me. Although I did. I cared a lot.

And then when he asked me to dance with him at the Harvest Dance, since everyone was sort of switching partners, I just acted all aloof and like, *Well, okay, I suppose I could dance with you, just this one time though.* I suppose I was kind of like playing hard to get, which seemed to make him more and more interested.

"I don't remember ever seeing you around school before," he told me as we danced a slow dance. "Until you made cheerleader anyway. Where you been hiding all this time?"

I shrugged. "I've been around."

And so it went. A regular cat-and-mouse game. But he thought he was the cat pursuing the hard-to-get mouse. Little did he know.

Still, I never dreamed that he would really pursue me seriously—at least not so quickly anyway. But the very next day, he called me and then came over to my house. He told me that he'd been postponing his breakup with Shawna, but the time had finally come. He actually seemed a little disturbed about the whole thing, which I thought was rather sweet. But I tried to console him and assure him that if it were really time to break up, the best thing was to just do it, and as quickly and painlessly as possible.

Maybe I was wrong about that part. Or maybe I'm just one of those people who has to learn everything the hard way.

two

"WHY DON'T YOU JUST KILL HER WITH KINDNESS?" MY MOM SUGGESTED as I hurried to consume my one slice of whole wheat toast and orange juice.

"Huh?" Now, Mom and I had been talking about my Shawna dilemma, which just shows how desperate I am. But I felt sure I must've missed something, because I was confused about what Mom was suggesting here. "You want me to *kill* her?"

My little brother, Tommy, seated at the breakfast bar, paused from munching his brightly colored cereal in order to make a loud exploding noise. Sometimes I think he and his ten-year-old friends are determined to destroy the world. "Blow her up!" he shouted without the slightest idea of what we were discussing.

"Eat your breakfast," I told him.

Mom laughed as she arranged some rust-colored chrysanthemums along with some autumn leaves in an old-fashioned milk can. I suspect she was going to use this as subject matter, because she's been back into her painting ever since school started. My mother is seasonal like that. Almost as good as a calendar. In the springtime, she haunts the local nursery and plants flowers in every available spot, including old boots and teapots. Then throughout the summer, she collects, trades, restores, and sells antiques. You can hardly make your way through our garage. Then it's painting in the fall, and some new form of crafts during the winter. Last year she took up knitting and made sweaters for everyone in our family. Mine had sleeves that would've worked for a baboon. But she meant well.

Mom came over and pushed a lock of hair from my forehead. "I'm only saying that you should be so nice to Shawna that she can't help but forgive you. Take her flowers or chocolate or a Hallmark card."

I rolled my eyes at her. "Yeah, like that'd work."

"Well, use whatever it is that Shawna's into. Just be so kind to her that whatever bad feelings she's having toward you will simply fade away and die. Kill her with kindness, Jordan."

"What are you talking about?" asked my twelve-year-old sister, Leah, as she made her usual late appearance. "Who are you going to kill?"

"None of your business," I told her as I downed my juice and headed back upstairs before she could beg me for a ride to school. Leah seems to think that now that I'm driving my own car, I should become her personal chauffeur. *Not.*

But I did consider Mom's idea as I slipped my homework into my bag. I wondered what I could possibly give to Shawna, the girl who has everything—well, besides Timothy. Really, what could help us get past this nasty jealousy business? Flowers or chocolate or cards would not even begin to cut it. Too lame. I glanced around my room desperately, knowing that it was time to be heading out. Then I noticed my collection of old vinyl LP albums. Shawna had been totally blown away by them the first time she'd been to my house.

"Where did you get all these?" she'd inquired as she carefully, almost reverently, leafed through the selection of Beatles albums.

"I thought they were kind of cool so I begged my dad to give them to me," I told her. "He's always been into music, and he bought most of these back when he was in high school. But now he just listens to the remastered versions on CDs."

"Man, you've got some good ones in here, but I'll bet these Beatles albums are really valuable."

"I don't know. They're not in that great of shape, and the jackets are kind of dog-eared."

"Well, they're totally cool."

So even though I was running late, I dug through my stack of LPs and picked out all the Beatles albums, slipped them into a nice shopping bag from Nordstrom, and put them in the backseat of my VW Bug.

I figured I'd wait until after school to present them to Shawna, maybe with a note expressing, once again, how very sorry I was for hurting her—because I *am* sorry. And if I really thought there was the slightest chance for her and Timothy to get back together, I would totally step out of the picture. At least I think I would. But then it's hard to be perfectly honest with yourself when it comes to matters of the heart.

Anyway, when I got to school, I decided to try out my mom's "kill her with kindness" advice during the course of the day as well. I mean, what could it possibly hurt?

"Hi, Shawna," I said in a cheerful voice, walking right up to where she was standing with Amber and Ashley. "I really like your top. Is it new?"

All three girls looked at me curiously.

"Yeah," Shawna answered with a skeptical expression. And I could tell she was thinking, *And what's it to you?*

"I thought so," I said. "Is it from Banana Republic? I thought I saw a top like that just last week. In fact I really wanted to get it myself."

Shawna narrowed her eyes. "Maybe you'd like to steal *this* from me too."

I nodded. "I guess I deserve that."

Amber looked like she was suppressing a smile now. And Ashley looked like she thought I was totally losing it.

"But really, it looks great on you, Shawna," I said. "Goes good with your eyes." Then, thinking I better not lay this on too thick, I made what I hoped was a graceful exit.

The next time I saw Shawna was at lunch. Timothy had gone with his buddies to listen to some college recruiter in the counseling center, so I was on my own for lunch today. Acting like nothing whatsoever was wrong, I went over to the table where the cheerleaders like to sit and I sat down right next to Shawna. "Mind if I join you?" I asked with a big smile.

She just shrugged.

"Thanks. It's kind of lonely eating by myself."

"How come you're not with *Tim?*" I could hear the cutting edge in her voice.

Now I shrugged. "Hey, I've got to have a life too." Okay, maybe that wasn't 100 percent true, but it wasn't exactly a lie either.

"Crud, I forgot to get a straw," said Shawna.

"Here, take mine," I offered her my still-unopened straw.

She gave me a sideways glance and then took the straw and mumbled a barely audible thanks.

The table was unusually quiet, and I could tell that everyone there was watching us, like they were waiting for some terrible catfight to break out at any moment. I could imagine the crowd gathered around us, cheering (probably for Shawna) as the two of us rolled around the floor clawing and scratching each other like wild animals. Thankfully, neither of us are really like that. At least we haven't been so far.

"Look," I said to no one in particular. "Is it okay with everyone here if Shawna and I just bury the hatchet?"

"Hey, that's what I'm hoping for," said Amber. "But how do you feel about it, Shawna?"

Shawna sighed. "I'm thinking about it."

"Great," said Amber. "I know it would make my life a whole lot easier."

Somehow we made it through lunch without any hair pulling or even name calling, but my stomach felt like it was tied up in a hundred knots by the time I dumped my tray of mostly uneaten food. I was thinking if stress doesn't kill you, I suppose it might at least help you lose weight.

After school, before cheerleading practice, I asked Shawna if I could talk to her privately in the parking lot.

Her eyes narrowed. "What? Are you going to try to beat me up out there or something?"

I laughed. "Yeah, you bet, Shawna." Like 90 percent of the other girls, she's several inches taller than me.

Anyway, I think curiosity got the best of her and she actually agreed to come out to my car with me.

"I have something for you," I told her as we approached my old VW Bug. "It'll probably seem kind of lame, but maybe you could just consider it my peace offering. You know, my way of showing you that I'm really and truly sorry for hurting you." I unlocked my car and pulled out the bag. "Here."

She looked in the bag and then back at me. "Are you serious?"

I nodded.

"Wow."

I felt hope surge through me. "Do you like them?"

"Of course. But are you sure?"

"Yes. Like I said, it's my way of saying sorry."

She almost smiled. "Well, thanks."

I wish we could've hugged or something spectacular like that. But at least she accepted my little offering, and I think we're on the road to recovery now. I have to admit it wasn't easy letting those Beatles albums go like that, but if it helps to mend things with Shawna, it's worth it.

I told Timothy about it when he called me tonight, and he thought I was totally crazy.

"You gave Shawna your Beatles albums?" he said for the second time, sounding like I'd given her one of my kidneys or something.

"I just wanted to do something to help us all move on, and I knew how much she liked them."

"Hey, I'd have liked them too."

I laughed. "Well, sorry, Tim. But I guess it's partly your fault that I had to make that kind of sacrifice."

"You mean because I couldn't stay away from you?" I could hear the smile in his voice now. Even over the phone I get this warm rush when he talks like that. It's the first time I've ever felt like this. I mean, I've had other boyfriends, but it always felt more like a game to me. This feels serious, like Timothy is The One. Now, I know that sounds pretty lame since I'm only sixteen. And I'd never admit it to anyone, not yet anyway, but I could imagine spending the rest of my life with this guy.

"Yeah," I said. "Shawna told me she wouldn't have been so mad if we hadn't gotten together so soon after the breakup."

"Don't be so sure," he said. "Knowing Shawna, we could've waited a whole month before we started dating and she still would've been furious. She's kind of possessive like that."

"Well, I think the worst is over now."

And I really do. I even think that Shawna and I might actually be able to become friends again. Anyway, I hope so. And I'm willing to go out of my way to try. Because, despite everything that's gone on, I really do like Shawna, and I'd love to have her as my best friend again. If we can only get past this Timothy thing. I'm thinking this could all really improve if she'd just start dating someone else. Now who could the lucky guy be? I think I'll start making a list of possibilities.

three

Well, chalk one up for Mom. She was right on about the kindness thing. Shawna Frye has not only forgiven me but we've actually been hanging together all week too. She even gave me a ride to the game last night, although I did ride home with Timothy.

"I don't see why you guys have to be best buddies now," he complained after I told him I couldn't go out with him Saturday.

"It's important," I tried to explain. "Shawna and I still have stuff to work through. Having her spend the night will help us to, you know, sort of heal our relationship."

He groaned. "Man, you sound like one of those daytime pop-psychology dudes, Jordan."

"Sorry, Tim, but just wait and see. It'll be worth it when Shawna and I are completely beyond this. Everyone will be able to get on with their lives without all the drama and stress."

He laughed. "Yeah, maybe you two will become best friends again and then we can become a happy little threesome."

"Real funny."

Now, I know he was just joking, but I have to admit that "threesome" image sent a chill down my spine. Suddenly I was wondering if this make-everything-cool-with-Shawna idea was getting a little out of hand. I would have to get a move on and find her another boyfriend. Soon. But then she came over on Saturday and we just hung out and basically had a great time together, just like we used to do before the Harvest Dance. And I realized that, as hard as it was, accomplishing this was probably worth putting Timothy off for one night.

I tried to explain all that to him on Sunday, and fortunately he seemed to understand. And we actually had a really great time. We went to a movie that turned out to be pretty good and then got a bite to eat and everything was cool. It only started to unravel on the way home. It was getting late and I'd told him that I had to be home by ten since it was a school night. My parents are pretty old-fashioned about curfews, and I know that if I break mine I will suffer, as in I won't be able to go out for a week, maybe two, depending on how late I am. And since I like having my little bit of freedom, I try to make it home on time.

But that wasn't the only problem. Okay, let me explain. Timothy is, shall we say, *romantic*. Oh, maybe that's not the right word. Maybe he's just very physical. Anyway, he really likes to make out. Now, to be perfectly honest, this is kind of new territory for me. I mean, I've kissed boys before. I actually had my first kiss when I was only thirteen, and really it wasn't any big deal. And like I said, I've had a few boyfriends, but never anything you could call serious. Although we'd hold hands and kiss, that was about it. Not that I'm a prude. At least I don't think I am. But for some reason I've gotten this idea that you really shouldn't go too far. Kara Hendricks and I used to talk about this a lot back when we were best friends. We both felt like guys wouldn't respect us if we went too far. But more than that, we both agreed that we wouldn't respect ourselves either.

Anyway, on the way home, Timothy decided to stop at the park. "Just to walk around and get some fresh air," he said.

"It'll have to be a quick walk," I told him, since it was already close to ten.

Well, the moon was out and everything seemed pretty romantic, and I was actually enjoying myself. We were just walking along, holding hands and doing a little bit of smooching here and there, and suddenly — like, what hit me? — we were just really going at it. I mean, his mouth was all over my mouth and it was like we were just starving for each other.

And somehow Timothy had me pushed up against the trunk of a tree. Not in an aggressive way though. Just really, really passionately. And to be honest, I was getting into it too. I liked the feeling of his body pressed against mine. It was exciting and I could feel those hormones rushing through me. Okay, I wasn't exactly thinking "hormones" at the time. I was more like thinking, *Oh, man, oh, man!* But suddenly I remembered what time it was. Plus I was feeling, shall we say, a bit overwhelmed. I kind of pushed him away (no easy task since he's about a foot taller than I am) and, catching my breath, told him, "Timothy, I have to get home. Now!"

"Oh, baby," he moaned in that deep voice that literally gives me goose bumps. "Don't do this to me."

"I'm sorry, Tim, but seriously, I'll get grounded if I'm not home by ten."

"Grounded?" He sounded kind of irritated now. "You gotta be kidding."

"Yeah. I know it probably sounds lame to you since you're a senior and probably get to do whatever you want. But remember, I'm still a sophomore and my parents are determined to keep me under their thumbs."

I grabbed him by the hand and pulled him back onto the path. "Come on, let's go."

He was pretty quiet on the short drive to my house, and I could tell something was bugging him. Then he parked his car, turned off the ignition, and looked at me.

"Hey, I'm sorry, Jordan," he said in a quiet voice. "I guess I was kind of a jerk tonight."

"That's okay," I told him, reaching for the door handle.

"No, it's not." He leaned over and kissed me. "Really, I'm sorry."

Then he walked me to the front door, and it felt like things were pretty much back to normal when we said goodnight. Now, if only my parents weren't sitting in there watching the clock.

"How was the movie?" asked my dad as he looked up from his book, which as usual was a thriller. My dad works for the city and I suppose he reads thrillers to break up the boredom.

"Okay," I told him, relieved that he hadn't mentioned my curfew. Then, suddenly, I felt self-conscious, as if he somehow knew what Timothy and I had just been doing in the park. And maybe he did. I mean, he used to be a teenager once himself, like a long, long time ago. But somehow I still find this hard to believe. Just the same, I decided to avoid the chance that he might start some kind of inquisition.

"How was your date, Jordan?" my mom called from the kitchen. I went in there and found her at the big oak table, paintbrush in hand as she peered down at a nearly finished painting.

"It was pretty good," I told her as I searched the interior of the fridge for something to eat. As usual, there was nothing terribly spectacular in there, so I settled for an apple.

"That looks nice," I told her as I looked over her shoulder at the painting. As I'd predicted, it was the fall flowers in the milk can.

"How's Timothy?" she asked as she set down her paintbrush and turned to look at me.

"Okay." I took a bite of my apple and attempted to look nonchalant.

"You know he's a lot older than you, Jordan."

"Just two years, Mom."

"I know, but that's a lot at this stage of your life."

I frowned at her. "Dad's like five years older than you."

She smiled. "But those are dad years. That's different."

I took another bite of my apple, slowly chewed, and then said, "So, what are you getting at?"

"Just that I don't want to see you getting in over your head."

"Over my head?"

"With Timothy."

"What exactly do you mean?"

"Oh, Jordan, you know what I mean. I don't want you getting so involved that you get hurt."

"How would I get hurt?" I was starting to feel slightly defensive now. "If you're really that worried about his age, Mom, well, think about this: Timothy's a lot more mature than boys my age. I mean, Timothy really cares about me. It's not like he's going to do anything to hurt me."

"Well, I hope not." Mom smiled. "And I want you to feel free to talk to me about this, Jordan. If there's anything I can do to help you, or if you have—"

"I've got homework," I told her quickly. I sensed we were about to go into the sex-talk arena again. And believe me, I did *not* need to go there tonight—at least not with a parental unit leading the discussion. I mean, I do love my mom, but sometimes she just doesn't get it. She thinks everything is about sex and "just saying no." But really, it's not that simple. Ask anyone.

I went up to my room and tried to do my homework, but my

mind just kept wandering. I really did want to talk to someone about what happened with Timothy tonight. It's not like it was that upsetting or anything, but I just wanted a sounding board. I realized that I obviously couldn't call Shawna. I mean, how tacky would *that* be? I considered my other friends, like Ashley or Amber or even Jenny, but then realized I just don't feel that close to them yet.

I considered my old (or is it ex?) best friend, Kara Hendricks. We were still close when school started this year, and then she sort of pulled away when I made cheerleader. I tried to bring her into my new circle of friends, but it was like she just couldn't handle it. We drifted apart. But I have to admit, I still miss her sometimes. She was always a great listener and I knew she cared about me—not because of who I was or who I hung with, but simply because we'd been friends for like forever. I wondered if it would be totally lame to call her now. I mean, after all, it was past ten thirty, and she and I had barely spoken in weeks. But then I wondered, why not? What could she do now that she's turned into this flaming Christian Jesus freak? She has to be nice, right? And so, without having to look it up, since I still know it by heart, I dialed her number.

"Sorry to call so late," I told her.

"Is something wrong?" she asked.

"No. I just need to talk. Do you mind?"

"No, that's okay. I'm the only one still up. I was just watching this news show about how this guy in Vermont, who'd been adopted at birth, accidentally married his birth sister."

"Gross." I shuddered.

"Yeah, tell me about it. So, what's up, Jordan?"

I could hear the curiosity in her voice, like she was trying to figure out why I was suddenly calling her up right out of the blue. "Well," I began, "I went out with Timothy tonight."

"And?"

"Well, we were having a really good time and we stopped by the park—"

"To make out?"

"Well . . ."

"And?"

"Yeah, we were making out. And, Kara, it was so cool. I mean, I have never felt like that before. It's like I'm on fire when he touches me, and my head literally starts to spin."

"Kind of like that girl in the old *Exorcist* movie?"

"Very funny."

"Sorry, go ahead."

"Anyway, it's like Timothy would probably just keep going, you know? I mean, like I can tell he really wants more."

"And what do you want?"

"Well, I don't know. I guess that's why I feel sort of confused. I mean, I *do* want more. But then I think maybe it's not right. And . . . oh, I don't know, I just really needed to talk to someone."

"Uh-huh."

I could hear this crunching noise. "Are you eating something?" I asked her.

"Just some stale Cheese Nips that Bree left out on the coffee table. They're pretty pathetic really."

"Oh. So, what do you think, Kara?"

"About you and Timothy having sex?"

"Sheesh. You don't exactly beat around the bush, do you?"

She laughed. "Well, isn't that what you're talking about?"

"I guess."

"Okay, this is what I think: I think I wouldn't want to have sex with a guy that I'd only been going with for a couple of weeks. For

27

that matter, I might not want to have sex with anyone that I wasn't married to."

"Really? You honestly believe you'll wait that long, Kara?"

"I don't know. It's not like I've been getting lots of offers lately."

"But seriously, do you really think you could wait until your wedding day?"

"Maybe."

"Is it because you're a Christian now?"

"Maybe. I still have a lot of things to sort out, Jordan. But I think Jesus says to take it one day at a time. And fortunately I don't have to make any sex decisions today."

"Well, I don't either. I just wanted someone to talk to. And you've always been a good listener."

"Uh-huh."

"I've patched things up with Shawna."

"Yeah, I noticed you two were hanging out last week. That's good to hear, Jordan."

"She says that she's over Timothy now, but it's hard to tell if she really means it."

"Do you think you could get over him that easily?"

I was stumped. Could I?

"I mean, you've only been going with him a couple of weeks, Jordan, and here you are, ready to jump into bed with him."

"I'm not going to jump into bed with him!"

"Well, you know what I mean. Do you think you'd get over him as quickly as Shawna did?"

"I don't know. The truth is, I think I like him more than Shawna ever did."

"Seriously?"

"Yeah. I never told you because I knew it would sound so lame, but I had a crush on him for most of last year."

"You're kidding."

"No. And I can tell he has really deep feelings for me too."

"After only a couple of weeks?"

"Yeah. It's like we're meant to be. It's hard to explain, but it just feels so amazing when I'm with him."

"You mean horny?"

I rolled my eyes. Maybe this call had been a bad idea. "*Nooooo.* It's more than that, Kara. Maybe you'd understand if you had a serious boyfriend."

Kara didn't respond, and suddenly I wondered if I'd hurt her feelings. "I'm sorry, Kara. That was really low. Are you still hanging out with that kid from art class? What's his name?"

"Edgar?"

"Yeah. What a weird name."

"Did you know his full name is Edgar Allen Peebles? His mom's name was Raven, like in that Edgar Allen Poe story."

"I'm sorry, Kara, but that is just too weird."

Kara laughed. "I think it's kind of cool. But for your information, Edgar and I are just really good friends. And that's good enough for me. In fact, I'm thinking if I ever were to get serious with a guy, I'd rather we were just good friends first."

"I don't think that's even possible, Kara."

"Anything's possible with God."

"Oh, brother." And on that note, I decided to bring this dead-end conversation to a halt. I can't believe I went looking for love advice from Kara. She may be sweet and actually pretty smart, but believe me, that girl is totally clueless when it comes to guys.

four

JUST WHEN YOU THINK YOU CAN FINALLY RELAX, LIKE LIFE IS ACTUALLY returning to normal, the roof totally caves in.

Shawna and I had been doing just fine, thank you very much. We'd been hanging together for a couple of weeks, not best friends exactly, since the thing with Timothy was still sort of between us. But I could imagine us becoming best friends again eventually, and I wanted for us to become best friends again, because I really do like her. (Okay, I *used* to like her.)

Anyway, despite our incredible losing streak in football, we cheerleaders ended the season on a happy note, and even Amber acted like she was proud of Shawna and me for patching things up. Life was good.

But life as I knew it ended last night. Let me explain.

To celebrate the end of our lackluster football season, Ashley Crow decided to have a party at her house on Saturday night. Her parents had conveniently left town for the weekend to visit friends in Clayburg. And, of course, they assumed that their only daughter would be mature and responsible while they were away. *Not.*

Let me tell you, Ashley is one gutsy girl. I would never dream of trying to pull off something like that if my parents were gone for the weekend. For one thing, my younger siblings would squeal on me. But besides that, I just don't have that kind of nerve. Still, I have to say I admired Ashley for her verve. (I think that's French for "boldness," although I dropped French after only one term, so I can't say for sure.)

Anyway, to my recent relief, Shawna had been showing some interest in Brett Hawkins (our good-looking but not-so-talented quarterback). Of course, I was encouraging her along these lines. I mean, first of all, Brett is a great guy. Oh, he's not Timothy, but he's not exactly Edgar Peebles either, if you know what I mean. Naturally, I thought that if Shawna had a new boyfriend, it would really improve our friendship and, well, sort of lighten things up all around.

So, on Saturday, Shawna and I went to the mall together and had a really great day. I even let her buy this totally cool sweater that I had spotted first. It was the only one in the store in size small, and I really, really wanted it. But I could see that Shawna wanted it too, so I just backed off and let her get it. Talk about self-sacrificing. Although, I do think it was just a little too snug on her and would've fit me perfectly. Not that I'm real skinny, because, believe me, I'm not. But Shawna's quite a bit taller, so anyway . . . but I digress. The thing is, I let her get it. My first mistake.

Then we came back to my house and hung out some more. I'd gotten this new Avril Lavigne CD that we wanted to listen to while we did our nails and good stuff like that. And really we were basically having a great day.

Now, because Brett and Shawna had not officially hooked up (although it was looking good last night after the game), I had told Shawna she could go to the party with me so she wouldn't have to show up alone. Which meant I had to tell Timothy he'd just have to go stag and meet me there. My second mistake.

So Shawna and I arrived at the party right on time since we'd promised Ashley that we'd help her get things set up, although it looked like she already had everything under control—at least to start with. So we were just kind of hanging with her in the kitchen and talking, and pretty soon more kids started coming. It wasn't really too surprising that some kids were bringing various forms of alcohol with them. I've discovered this is pretty much the norm at these parties.

Even so, I must state that I am not a boozer. The pure and simple reason for this is that due to my size or metabolism or whatever, I simply cannot handle alcohol. I tried it a couple of times, just to be sociable, and it totally wiped me out, made me sicker than a dog, and then I couldn't even remember if I'd had fun or not. On top of that, I basically felt like crud for most of the next day. So, I've decided it's just not worth it. It doesn't particularly bother me when my friends indulge, and I've actually decided that I make a pretty good designated driver, although there are those who shall remain unnamed who think my driving skills could use a little improvement. Anyway, because there wasn't much to do yet, I just casually sipped my Sprite and kept an eye on the door for Timothy.

Meanwhile, Brett had arrived and seemed to be really putting the moves on Shawna. Not surprising, since Shawna looked pretty hot in that sweater, and I'm sure the snug fit didn't bother Brett a bit. But I was happy for them and smiling as I watched the two of them joking around, dancing and drinking together. And I was thinking, *All right, my troubles are over*. Like this should really cinch the deal for everyone. My third mistake. Good grief, how many mistakes did I make?

Timothy finally showed up with a couple of buddies, and the first thing I realized was that they'd already been drinking. But that didn't seem like such a big deal since these are hefty guys and usually able to hold their liquor, so to speak.

Well, to start with, Timothy and I were just hanging out like everything was cool, and it was. But I could tell by the way he was acting that he was expecting something from me. And to be perfectly explicit, and based on some suggestive conversations, I'm sure he was expecting *sex*.

Now, while I found this to be somewhat flattering (I mean, it's nice to be wanted), it was also making me a little uncomfortable. And I felt kind of self-conscious when he would start grabbing for me in, well, slightly conspicuous places (I don't mean *places* as in locations in the *house*, but *places* on my *body* that I'd just as soon not be touched, at least not in public). And I honestly don't think he'd have been so bold and pushy if he hadn't been drinking. But I could be wrong. I've been known to be wrong.

"Timothy!" I said for like the umpteenth time, carefully removing his hand from where it had wandered. "Behave yourself."

"What's wrong?" he asked, looking seriously hurt.

I glanced around the noisy and increasingly crowded room. "People are watching."

Well, he just laughed. "Hey, look around, Jordan. No one gives a rip about what we do."

"I give a rip," I told him and knew I sounded prissy, even to myself.

"You wanna go someplace more private?" he said in this lowered voice that normally thrills me.

I actually considered his suggestion for a moment. I mean, I did like the idea of having all of Timothy's attention to myself, and I did really like him. But at the same time, there was something about the way he was acting—not to mention the smell of something a whole lot stronger than beer on his breath — that made me hesitate. I suppose that was my fourth mistake.

It was then that Timothy let go of me and flopped down into an easy chair in the corner of the living room, but I could tell he wasn't happy with me. So I went over and sat down on the arm of the chair. I started playing with his hair, hoping I could cheer him up. He has the best hair — thick and blond and cut short, but not too short. Just perfect. Then he pulled a silver flask out of his jacket pocket.

"Want some?" he asked, holding it in my direction with a slightly sloppy, but undeniably cute, grin.

"No thanks." I patted him on the cheek.

He rolled his eyes. "Yeah, it figures."

He took a long swig, and then another. We sat there for what seemed like quite a while without talking or anything, and I was starting to get pretty uncomfortable because it almost seemed like I had totally disappeared as far as Timothy was concerned.

I finally turned around to see what he was so captivated by and realized that he had his eyes focused on Shawna and Brett, who slow-danced in full embrace to what was actually a fast song.

Then, in that same instant, Timothy stood up and walked right up to them. He tapped Brett on the shoulder like the way people used to do back in the old days when they wanted to cut in. Of course, Brett and Shawna both looked pretty surprised. Brett said something to Timothy, and although I couldn't hear it, I suspected by Brett's expression that he was telling Timothy to back off.

But that's when I saw this look in Shawna's eyes. Now, how would I describe that look? Maybe like a hungry cat or perhaps a tiger who sees raw meat. Then she turned and said something to Brett, who then frowned and just walked away. And the next thing I knew, Shawna and Timothy were dancing together — slow-dancing just like she'd been doing with Brett, even though the song was still fast.

Now, I can't even begin to describe the millions of emotions that surged through me in that instant. First of all, I was hurt, deeply hurt. But then I was embarrassed too. More like humiliated. But then I told myself to just chill, be mature. Timothy was probably just dancing with Shawna for old time's sake. I told myself to be a good sport about it. Before long, I'd be the one dancing with Timothy again. But when they danced right into the next song, I realized I was in serious trouble. I went into the kitchen to get away from the crowd and the music.

"What's up with Tim and Shawna?" asked Ashley as she refilled a bowl with cheese puffs.

"I don't know."

She shook her head. "Looks to me like they're patching things up."

Amber came in. She put a hand on my shoulder and said, "Now, don't you go falling apart on us, Jordan. You knew when you started going with Timothy that this could happen."

"I did not!" I turned and glared at her.

Amber laughed. "Come on, Jordan, don't play stupid. You know good and well what goes 'round comes 'round, and you should've known that Shawna wouldn't let Timothy go without putting up a good fight."

"But Shawna and I are friends," I began.

"Good," said Amber. "Let's keep it that way. But if Shawna and Timothy get back together, I don't want to hear any whining or complaining out of you."

"But—"

"No buts," said Amber as she popped an orange cheese puff into her mouth. "All's fair in love and war. Right, Jordan?"

Well, I had no answer for that, and feeling embarrassingly close to tears, I decided to just split. Maybe that was my fifth mistake. I'm not sure. Maybe I'll never know for sure. All I knew was that I had to get out of that house before I said or did something really, really stupid. So I jumped in my Bug and put the pedal to the metal. It's too bad that Bugs aren't designed to go faster. I could've made a really spectacular exit.

five

I DIDN'T WANT TO GO HOME YET. IT WAS BARELY TEN AND MY CURFEW ON nonschool nights isn't until eleven thirty, so I drove over by the high school—don't ask me why—and then I noticed the apartment complex that Kara lives in. I knew it was a little late for an unexpected visit, but I drove over there anyway, and to my complete and utter relief, Kara was climbing out of this big old black Cadillac that I swear looked just like a Mafia car.

"Kara!" I screamed out my window as the car pulled away.

"Jordan?" She peered over at my car.

I parked my car with one wheel on the sidewalk and then leaped out and ran over to her, literally falling into her arms as I sobbed uncontrollably. Okay, so what if I am a bit of a drama queen at times? Tonight I had good reason.

"What's wrong?" she asked as I continued to sob. "Is it your parents? Did someone die? Jordan, what is it?"

"It's, it's Timothy," I cried.

"Is he okay? Did he get hurt?"

"He's with Shawna. They're, they're dancing." I felt Kara try to hide a giggle, and feeling a little silly I stepped away. "It was awful," I told her, looking down at my feet. "I just need to talk to someone."

She shook her head in this dismal sort of way, and I suspect she was thinking I was a total idiot, and maybe I am, but then she invited me to come up to her apartment to talk.

I was relieved that her mom and sister were both out. Sometimes I think Kara is so lucky because she has such a small family (only three of them all together) and so she has the apartment, which is really pretty cool with its contemporary furnishings and her dad's modern art, to herself a lot.

"Maybe it's for the best," she finally said as she handed me a cup of green tea.

"The *best?*" I cried. "How can it be for the best, Kara? I think I *love* him."

She sat down and looked at me. "Does he love *you?*"

I shrugged. "He'd been drinking tonight."

She nodded. "So, he'd been drinking and started flirting with his old girlfriend?"

"Yeah."

"Sounds like a really great guy, Jordan."

"He is," I insisted. "You just don't know him like I do. When it's just the two of us and we're talking . . . well, it's like we're the only two people in the world. He's not really like the guy you see in school. He's actually got a very sweet, sensitive side."

"Obviously."

I studied her closely, wondering since when she had become so outspoken and opinionated. In fact, I wanted to ask her but felt certain she'd include "Jesus" in her answer, and frankly I just didn't want to hear anything like that tonight.

"I'm sorry," she said.

Well, that's better, I was thinking. But I just nodded my head in the most pitiful manner, hoping I might be able to garner just a bit more sympathy.

"It's too bad that you had to get hurt, Jordan," she continued. "But you never know, something good might come out of it."

"Something good?" I demanded. "Like what?"

"Oh, I don't know. But when I went through something hard"—she peered at me in this sort of way that made me think that "something" had to do with me and then continued—"well, it made me grow up in some ways, and it made me realize that I needed Jesus in my life."

I held up my hands. "Listen, Kara, I just had my heart stomped on tonight. I do not think I can handle a sermon right now."

She just shrugged. "Whatever."

So we just sat there in silence, and finally I realized that Kara was just not going to get this. If I wanted sympathy, I had come to the wrong place.

"Thanks for the tea," I told her as I stood up. "I better go."

"I'll be praying for you," she said with a smile.

I rolled my eyes at her. "Yeah, whatever trips your trigger, Kara."

And then I left. But instead of going home like a smart girl, I decided to drive back by the party. Okay, I'm almost losing count here, but I think that was my sixth mistake.

Of course, the party was still going strong, and there were cars and kids everywhere. The music was blasting out through the open doors, and I could see that Ashley's house was getting a little trashed.

I decided to go through the back door to the kitchen and make as inconspicuous an entrance as possible. And for some reason, I began to get this hopeful feeling, like maybe Timothy had quit dancing with Shawna by now. And perhaps he'd noticed I was missing and gone looking for me. I imagined him apologizing to me with big sad eyes, telling me the dance with Shawna was just a fluke, that his judgment had been impaired from drinking and that it would never ever happen again. Maybe Shawna and Brett had even left the party together, driven to Reno, and gotten married or something. Okay, call me a perennial optimist, but I felt like it could happen.

As I was going in the back door, Ashley was coming out. She was carrying an area rug, held out at arm's length, and had a very sour expression on her face.

"What's wrong?" I asked.

"Everything," she snapped as she tossed the rug out the door.

"What's going on?" I asked.

"It's a disaster, Jordan," she told me. "Kids I don't even know keep crashing the party, and they're all acting like total pigs. Betsy just puked on my mom's Oriental carpet." Her voice broke like she was about to cry.

"Can I help you?" I offered, not even sure what I could actually do. To be honest, I just wanted to find Timothy and get out of there.

"Would you?" Her eyes grew hopeful.

"What can I do?"

"Help me start clearing the place out. Maybe we could say my parents are coming home."

"Or that someone called the police," I suggested, half worried that it could actually happen. I wasn't sure how my parents would react if they knew I was at a party like this, even if I hadn't been drinking.

"That's it," she said. "But I can't say that myself, since this is my party. Oh, Jordan, could you go out there and start telling kids, kind of quiet you know, so that it seems real?"

I shrugged. "Sure, why not?"

She hugged me. "Thanks, Jordan. You're my hero."

So I went out into the crowd of people, most of whom I didn't even know, but as I spotted my friends, I began telling them with wide eyes and a slightly frightened expression that I'd heard the party was going to get busted any minute. And let me tell you, it was amazing how the word just spread like wildfire, and pretty soon the whole house, at least the downstairs, was evacuated.

"You are a lifesaver, Jordan," said Ashley as she started picking up empties and dropping them into a trash bag.

"I think there are still some kids upstairs," I told her.

"Wanna go tell them there's a raid going on?"

Getting into the spirit even more, I ran upstairs and started flinging doors open. "The police are coming!" I shouted. "This party's getting busted." It was actually kind of fun, although a bit eye-opening, as I was finding kids everywhere in all kinds of "compromising" positions. But when I discovered Timothy and Shawna in the master bathroom, of all places, and actually doing *it* right there in the sunken tub, I thought I was going to literally die. Without even saying a word, I just turned around and went downstairs in a state of shock.

"What's wrong?" asked Ashley when she saw me. "It looks like you saw a ghost. Oh, crud, please tell me you didn't find a dead body up there somewhere!"

I just shook my head and, in the same moment, Timothy and Shawna came flying down the stairs, the last ones to leave. Timothy hadn't even bothered to fasten his belt, and Shawna had her new sweater on backward. They were barely out the door when I started to sob all over again.

Then to my complete surprise, Ashley put her arms around me and gave me the warmest hug. "Oh, poor Jordan," she said soothingly. "Those two are such total jerks, I think they deserve each other. Just forget about them, Jordan."

And finally I stopped crying, and feeling just a teeny bit better, I offered to help her clean up.

I could tell it was going to take a long time, and not wanting to get grounded on top of everything else, I decided to call my parents and actually tell them the truth. Okay, part of the truth.

"Ashley's party got totally crashed by a bunch of rowdy kids," I told my dad. "They brought alcohol and really trashed the place, and I want to help her clean up. But I think it's going to take a while. Maybe I should just spend the night."

"Now, where exactly does Ashley live?" my dad asked. And I could tell he was trying really hard to believe me. So I told him the address, fairly certain that before the night was over, he'd be driving his old Volvo by to make sure I was really there.

We worked until around two in the morning just to get rid of all the "evidence" of illegal or illicit activities, and let me tell you, it was totally gross. I was convinced by then that I would *never* throw a party when my parents were gone. At that point, we were so exhausted that we decided to call it a night and pick up where we'd left off in the morning.

Even though I was totally exhausted, both emotionally and physically, I stayed awake long after Ashley had crashed. All I could think about was the horrible scene I'd stumbled upon in the master bathroom. I think I cried myself to sleep.

six

SOMETIMES THERE'S NOTHING LIKE GOOD HARD WORK WHEN YOU'RE depressed. And believe me, I was seriously depressed the following day. It was probably a good thing that I spent most of the day helping Ashley put her house back together. It probably kept me from doing something else, something totally regrettable, like ramming my car into Shawna's.

"You're really good at this," Ashley told me as I helped her glue a lamp base that had been broken.

"It's my obsessive-compulsive side," I told her. "I like to make everything perfect. It's pretty sick, really. You should see my room."

She laughed. "Yeah, Shawna told us about it once." Then she got this startled expression. "I'm sorry, Jordan. I shouldn't have mentioned her."

"It's okay," I tried to reassure her. "I might as well get used to it." I studied Ashley for a moment. "So, did Shawna make fun of me when she told you about my impeccably neat room?"

Ashley kind of shrugged. "She said you have to keep everything in its place or you totally lose it."

I sighed. I should've known I couldn't trust Shawna, not even on the most basic levels. "Well," I said, "that's not completely true. But I am kind of a neat freak."

"Hey, I'm not complaining, Jordan. I don't know what I would've done without you. I owe you big-time, girl."

So, perhaps I've made a friend through all this. Although it's a small consolation, considering what I've lost. Mainly Timothy. I'm pretty sure that I've lost him. Now, I know I shouldn't care, since everyone except Shawna seems to think he's a total jerk anyway. And maybe he is, but that doesn't seem to stop the way I feel about him. I mean, I'm kind of experiencing a love-hate thing at the moment. But I can't stop thinking about him. It's like he's stuck in my heart somehow. I suppose it could simply be my obsessive-compulsive nature just caught in a groove and unable to get out. But I don't think so. I think it's just that I still love him.

Ashley and I finally finished our clean-a-thon by midafternoon. "Let me take you to lunch," offered Ashley. "It's the least I can do to thank you. And I have to stop by the mall to check on my mom's shop. I got someone else to fill in for me today, but I'd better make sure nothing's gone wrong over there."

I leaned back into the comfortable seat of Ashley's car. It's an almost-new Honda Accord and in much better shape than my old VW Bug. And Ashley had given me what was actually a pretty cool T-shirt to wear.

"Believe it or not, it used to fit me," she'd told me, laughing as she looked down at her well-endowed chest. "I'd only worn it once and then my mom accidentally washed it in hot water. We're talking serious ShrinkyDink. But I liked it so much that I couldn't stand to throw it away."

Personally, I was glad that she hadn't.

I turned and looked at Ashley as she drove toward town. I've never really thought about it much, since Ashley and I have never been real close before, but I could see now that she's actually very pretty with her straight auburn hair and big brown eyes.

"Have you ever been dumped like that, Ashley?" I asked as she turned toward the mall.

"Are you kidding?" she laughed. "Sheesh, lots of times."

"Really? I figured you'd be the one to do the dumping."

"Yeah, well, I've done that too."

"Did you ever get dumped by someone you really liked?"

She was quiet for about a minute and then nodded. "You probably don't remember, but Brett and I used to go out."

"Oh, yeah," I said. "I *do* remember that. What happened?"

She shrugged. "What usually happens?"

"Huh?"

"You know. Same old, same old."

"That's just it, Ashley," I told her rather emphatically. "I *don't* know. To be perfectly honest, I'm still kind of new at this."

She turned and looked at me and then smiled—a sincere smile. "You're really a sweet girl, Jordan. It's almost a shame."

I frowned. "A shame?"

"That you've gotten yourself mixed up in this crowd."

"Huh?" Now I was really feeling lost.

She sighed, and for some reason it reminded me of a sound that an old woman who was bone tired or perhaps just jaded by life might make. "Sometimes I just get so sick of high school, Jordan, that I think it'll be so great to finally graduate and get on with my life."

Now, I don't usually feel like that myself. I mean, usually—and especially this fall—I thought that high school was so cool that I wanted it to last, like, forever. But after what happened last night, I think maybe I understand what she's saying. "But at least you're a junior," I reminded her.

"Yeah, only a freaking year and a half until I get to escape." Then she laughed. "Sorry. I guess I'm still bummed about that stupid party." She shook her head as she turned into the mall parking lot. "Live and learn."

At lunch I probably went on a little too long about Timothy and Shawna, but Ashley was fairly patient with me, probably because I'd been so helpful in getting her house back together.

But finally she said, "You know, Jordan, you need to just let it go."

"Let it go?"

"Uh-huh. *Let it go.*"

"How do you do that?"

"You've just got to get on with your life."

"What if I can't?" I noticed I was biting the edge of a fingernail, something I thought I'd given up ages ago. I put my hands in my lap and looked at her.

"Well, then ask yourself, what good is it going to do to be consumed with jealousy?"

"Consumed with jealousy?" I echoed, wondering if that was really how I came across.

She nodded. "Yeah. That's how you seem to me, Jordan. It's like it's eating you alive that Shawna got Timothy back."

"But it was wrong," I told her. "It should be against the rules to use sex to get a guy back."

Well, this made Ashley laugh so hard that I thought she was going to wet her pants or split a gut. "The rules?" she finally sputtered. "*What* rules, Jordan? Don't you know there *are* no rules when it comes to this kind of thing?"

"Yeah, yeah." I rolled my eyes. "All is fair in love and war. But you'd think when people were friends—"

"Friends?" She looked at me like I was about three years old. "Did you really think that Shawna was your friend?"

"We used to be good friends—"

"No, I mean, after you moved in on her man. Did you honestly think she was your friend after *that?*"

I considered this.

"Get real, Jordan. Shawna was just using you, worming her way back into your world so she could get the upper hand and gain some control over what was going on with you and Timothy. Didn't you get that?"

I shook my head. Call me dumb or naive or just plain stupid, but I did *not* get that. "I thought she was my friend," I said in a mousy voice.

"It's how the game is played," she told me. "Sheesh, we've been playing it since middle school. I guess it really is new to you." She pushed her empty plate away from her. "I suppose that does put you at a serious disadvantage, Jordan."

"You're telling *me.*" I looked at her hopefully. "I'm open to any suggestions."

"That's just it. Like I was telling you, I'm getting kind of sick of the game. I mean, maybe you're just catching me on a bad day, but sometimes I just wish everyone would grow up."

Then I remembered something she'd said earlier. "But what about Brett Hawkins, Ashley? Would you lower yourself to play the game if you could get Brett back?"

She shrugged.

"You know that he and Shawna aren't going out now. Did you see him leave last night? He looked pretty bummed," I said.

"Oh, right," she said sarcastically. "Like I want to go get him on the freakin' rebound. You bet!"

"Yeah, I suppose that's not such a good idea."

"If Brett and I are meant to be, then fine. But I'm not going to chase him."

"Right." And I told myself I wouldn't go chasing Timothy either, but unfortunately I didn't exactly believe myself. We talked for a while longer, and I really tried to take her advice about letting things go. I even put on this happy mask face, like, *Hey, everything's cool.* But the pitiful truth is there is this little something inside me that just won't let it go.

Later that afternoon as I left Ashley's house, I couldn't help but drive by Shawna's place to see if Timothy's car was there, which it wasn't, and then by Timothy's house to see if he was home, which he wasn't. Naturally, that didn't make me feel any better because then I realized that the two of them might actually be out together, and that made me sick.

Then, even as I drove, quite slowly, toward home, I found myself craning my neck to peer down every single side street, searching for that familiar red Mustang classic that Timothy and his dad restored together. It's an easy car to spot, but I didn't see it anywhere. And, of course, this didn't make me feel one bit better.

I even started to dial Shawna's home number on my cell phone, thinking I'd just wait to see if she'd answer, planning to hang up if she did. But I remembered they have caller ID at her house and decided not to risk it. But I did consider finding a pay phone and calling from there. Now, I ask you, how lame is that?

seven

I SERIOUSLY THINK I'M BECOMING A STALKER. I SAW THIS SHOW ON TV once about these whacked-out people who get so obsessed with someone that they can't even control themselves anymore. They drive by some poor unsuspecting slob's house at all hours of the day and night. Sometimes they park out front and just sit and watch. There are actually laws against it in some states—maybe even ours. But, believe me, it's a sick, sick thing. It's been only five days since Timothy broke my heart, but the way I'm acting right now is seriously scaring me.

You see, I find myself using any excuse I can think of to drive my car around town. I'll take Tommy to Scouts or Leah to piano lessons or even go to the store for my mom. I'm surprised she's not suspicious.

But as soon as I've dropped off Leah or Tommy or picked up a gallon of 2-percent milk, I drive directly to Timothy's house. I slowly cruise by to see if he's home, and if he's not, I try to figure out where he might be. My first guess is usually Shawna's. And so I drive by there next. And on it goes.

I've even taken to using my parents' cars sometimes, like I'm going undercover. And I can't believe how much money I'm wasting on gas, not to mention that my homework is suffering. But it's like I don't even care about anything except how I can get Timothy back. I know, I know, I shouldn't want him back so badly. But I do. I can't even begin to explain why. Maybe it's because he's so doggone cute. Or maybe it's because he's the most popular jock in school and I think everyone will respect me more if I'm his girl. Or maybe I'm just mad at Shawna and I want to get even. Believe me, I've considered all these things. But what I keep coming down to is that it's just plain and simple love—*true* love. I mean, really, isn't it possible that what I feel is the real thing? And like they say in old movies, true love never runs smoothly.

So I've decided I'm not really a stalker, maybe since I don't want to do Timothy any harm, and I think that stalkers usually do want to hurt someone. I'm just trying to be opportunistic by putting myself in the right place at the right time. I envision us running into each other—well, not literally (although the thought has occurred to me before, like we have this unexpected collision and the next thing I know he's wiping blood from my forehead and gently kissing me), but mostly I mean running into each other somewhere that I just happen to be at the same time he is. And then we talk and apologize and patch things up, and we are happily back together again, maybe even picking out wedding rings and china patterns.

Although, I don't have the same nonviolent feelings toward Shawna. Sometimes I actually wish I *could* run into her, as in run her down in the middle of the street with my car—hopefully in her cheerleading uniform, leaving this big red and blue blob smeared across the pavement. Okay, not really, since that's totally gross, not to mention illegal and actually pretty evil. But sometimes I feel as if I'd really like to hurt her.

Because, believe me, *she is asking for it*. Every single day this week so far, and this is only Wednesday, Shawna has blatantly flaunted their relationship right in my face. Now, I've tried to take Ashley's advice to "just move on," at least as far as appearances go. And to the casual observer I'm sure that it looks like I have moved on since I go around wearing my little happy mask all day. I smile and laugh and carry on like my heart's still in one piece, but beneath it all, I am dying.

And does Shawna have one single ounce of sympathy for me? Does she care how I may be feeling? Forget about it! She is one twisted devil chick. I think about how careful I was of her feelings when Timothy and I were together, how I tried not to flaunt our relationship. Well, Shawna seems to get her kicks out of torturing me. Believe me, she's an expert at twisting the knife she so gracefully slipped into my back the night of Ashley's party.

"Timothy says that the basketball team is looking really good," she said to Amber at practice this afternoon, like anyone was asking. Of course, Shawna always saves these comments until she is absolutely sure I'm within earshot. "You should've seen their scrimmage last night," she continued loudly. "Timothy is playing better than ever. It was awesome. I wouldn't be surprised if we go to state this year."

I exchanged glances with Ashley and saw her mouth the word "chill" at me, but it was all I could do not to explode into a bazillion hot pieces. I guess I should be thankful for my expertise as a gymnast at times like that, because I simply walked away and acted like I was practicing a series of flips through the gym. Thankfully, it actually helped to relieve a little tension. Amber and Ashley gave me a nice little round of applause when I finished, and I put on my happy mask and gave them a flamboyant bow. I think I saw a slight scowl on Shawna's face just then, like perhaps she was worried that Jordan Ferguson still had it, like maybe I was still something of a threat to her. And consequently a small, barely perceptible ripple of satisfaction ran through me.

I suppose moments like that fuel the teeniest bit of hope in me. And I start to think that if I really applied myself I might be able to use my talents and charm and perseverance to get Timothy back. It encourages me to think that Shawna knows this too, and I think it worries her. But I refuse to make my move until I have a solid and foolproof plan.

But so far, I think the way I'm handling this is working for me. For one thing, I've garnered more support within the cheerleading circle. Everyone thinks I'm being a super good sport, and having Ashley solidly on my side hasn't hurt anything either. And it all seems to be making Shawna increasingly nervous.

Like yesterday at lunch, after I'd managed for a whole day and a half to act like everything was totally cool, Shawna finally pulled me aside and said, "We're okay, aren't we, Jordan?"

I forced a smile to my lips and just shrugged. "Why wouldn't we be?"

She laughed nervously. "Well, you know . . ."

"Hey," I said in my most nonchalant tone, taking a quick glance around to make sure that no one else could hear me. "If you have to have sex in a *bathtub* just to win Timothy back, well, you just go, girl." Then I slapped her on the back, laughed, and walked off to join Ashley. And I quickly told Ashley something completely unrelated but pretty funny, and we both threw back our heads and laughed. Ashley has the best laugh. It just rolls across the room like a bowling ball. Then I glanced back over to where Shawna was standing and gave her a look that suggested we had just enjoyed a joke about her.

I must admit I am slightly surprised by how mean I can be. I didn't used to be like this. Even when I noticed the hurt look in Shawna's eyes, I didn't care. If anything, I was glad. And even though I pretty much know exactly how she feels, I still don't feel sorry for her. Maybe I should be concerned that I could be turning into a totally selfish and heartless person. But mostly I'm not that worried, because what I did seems like *nothing* compared to what Shawna did to me. And, as Amber says, all is fair in love and war.

Speaking of love, Timothy did apologize to me on Monday. And I could tell he was really sorry too, like he'd been caught up in something that hadn't been his real intention.

"I feel really bad, Jordan," he told me in the parking lot after a full day in school, where it felt like he'd been avoiding me like the plague. I'd never thought of Timothy as a coward, but I suspect he felt pretty uncomfortable.

I stood up a little straighter, actually hopeful that this could be the moment I'd been waiting for. I looked into his eyes with an expression that I hoped conveyed just how deeply wounded I'd been. And his features seemed to soften as he looked down at me. I was thankful that I'd taken care to dress just right, every hair in place, makeup perfect.

"Yeah, I feel bad too," I told him in a very gentle voice.

"I honestly didn't mean for that to happen, Jordan. I guess I was just mad that you went to the party without me, and then I was drinking way too much. I never meant for things to turn out this way."

I shook my head in a sympathetic way. "Me neither."

"Because we really had something, Jordan," he continued. "You and me. I really felt like my relationship with you was different."

I nodded without speaking.

Then he shoved his hands into his letter jacket and looked up at the sky for a moment as if he was trying to figure things out. "But maybe it's for the best, you know?" He sighed deeply. "I mean, maybe it was just meant to be like this."

I felt a wave of disappointment break over me, but just the same, I managed to maintain my best poker face and simply said, "Maybe so, Tim."

"So, you're really okay with everything, Jordan?" He looked hopeful now, like he thought he was getting off the hook really easy. And I suppose after all Shawna had put him through a few weeks back, I must've seemed like a real pushover.

"Well, you really hurt me, Timothy," I told him. Now this was true enough. "And I guess you showed me that you're not the guy I thought you were."

He frowned slightly. Had I hit a nerve?

"So why should I have a problem if you want to go back to someone like Shawna?" I made a face like I was smelling a pair of dirty socks. And that's when I lied to him. "I mean, why would I want you back at all after that?" Then I kind of smiled in this sad way as I opened the door of my car. "Have a nice life, Timothy."

Somehow I managed to drive away in what I'm sure appeared a perfectly calm and controlled manner, but inside I was hurting and furious and actually seething by the time I was half a block away. And when I was two blocks away, I was actually screaming at the top of my lungs. Of course, I realized I had totally forgotten cheerleading practice after school. And so I pretended like I was simply driving to the local convenience store, where I went in and bought myself a huge Coke and a big package of Whoppers to share with the other girls. No one seemed to notice how hoarse my voice was at practice.

So this has been my little game plan—playing it cool—and so

far it is better than nothing and has probably kept me from totally losing it. But I still feel like I'm getting nowhere and I wonder if I need to take it up a notch or two.

As a result, I have to ask myself, *What does Timothy Lawrence really want?* I know he and I really had something, and although I must admit that a part of it was physical attraction, there was something more too. I mean, when we talked, we *really* talked. He confessed to me that he's worried about what happens after high school, and he can't decide which college to go to, and he's afraid he won't play ball well enough to get a scholarship. He told me sweet, sensitive things—things I'm sure he doesn't tell anyone else, things I would never dream of repeating. And I also remember him telling me, right after he broke up with Shawna, that their relationship had been empty and shallow and how he wanted something more—someone who really understood him, someone who knew how to listen and really care, something that he told me I had and Shawna didn't.

So after cheerleading practice I went home and made a list. I know I should've been studying for my history exam tomorrow, but somehow I just couldn't focus. Instead I made this list and taped it to the back of his picture, which I still keep on my dresser.

What Timothy Wants

1. A girlfriend who really listens to him. Someone who cares. Someone he can talk to about important things.

2. A girlfriend who's popular, since he's in with the "in" crowd.

3. A girlfriend who's available when he needs her around. He's one of those guys who really enjoys having a girl hanging on to him a lot of the time.

4. Lots of friends. He loves having his friends around him.

5. Lots of laughs. He likes being the center of attention.

6. *Fun. This is a guy who loves to have fun.*

7. *To star in basketball. He adores this sport.*

8. *To get a scholarship in basketball. It's possible.*

9. *To graduate. He told me he can't afford to lose a single credit this year.*

10. *To have sex. Okay, no beating around the bush here. This seems to be pretty important to him.*

And that was where my list abruptly ended—on number ten, *To have sex.* Wouldn't you know it?

In all fairness, Timothy isn't *just* about having sex. Like I said, we had a great time for more than two weeks of dating without ever feeling too much pressure to go to bed together. We talked and laughed and totally enjoyed being together. It was only toward the end of our short-lived relationship that this came up, which made me wonder, *Had he and Shawna been having sex all along?* Duh. Why hadn't I ever thought to ask her about this while we were still friends? Sheesh, I can be so totally naive sometimes.

And so I called Ashley. "Did Timothy and Shawna have sex?" I asked somewhat abruptly.

She laughed. "You're the one who caught them in the tub."

"No, I mean *before* that. When they were going out together *before* the Harvest Dance breakup."

A long pause. "Why are you asking me this?"

"I just want to know."

"What do *you* think, Jordan?"

"I think they did."

"Bingo."

Now I paused.

"Does it really matter, Jordan? I mean, I thought you had moved on and were just dealing with it. We've all been really proud of you."

I realized it was time to put on my happy mask again. "Yeah, I have moved on, Ashley. I guess I was just curious is all. Now I know. No big deal." And then I started asking her about her mom's shop in the mall. Ashley had told me that I could probably work there if I wanted, especially during the Christmas season.

"You really interested in a job?" she asked.

"Kind of. I wouldn't mind having some extra money. And it'd sure beat babysitting my little brother and sister."

Finally, sure that I had convinced her I wasn't obsessing about Timothy and Shawna, I hung up the phone and immediately began wondering how far I would really go to get Timothy back.

I flashed back to that scene of the two of them floundering around in that stupid oversized bathtub, and to be perfectly honest, it was pretty disgusting. But then it wouldn't have to be like that. Would it?

eight

I DON'T THINK I'VE EVER REALLY HATED ANYONE BEFORE. I MEAN, I REALLY disliked Miss Jones, my third-grade teacher, especially after she humiliated me by making me sit in the hallway for talking. But I don't recall experiencing this venomous emotion, the kind of thing I would describe as real honest-to-goodness hatred, that I presently feel toward Shawna Frye.

She completely and thoroughly disgusts me. I can barely stand the sight of her. Even the sight of her streaky blonde hair flashing down the hall makes me want to barf. Of course, she's not a real blonde, and judging by her roots I suspect that her natural hair color is kind of a boring, muddy brown. No wonder she wants to cover it up. She's such a phony. I don't see how Timothy can stand her. I cannot believe I ever considered her my friend or thought that I was hers. She is a manipulative, lying, stealing, cheating hypocrite. And it's plain to see she's still got her sights set on me.

I mean, isn't it bad enough that she stole Timothy from me? Any normal person would call it even at this point. But no, it's like she's got to keep this personal vendetta going. I think her goal is to knock me down so low that I will just tuck my tail between my legs and crawl under a rock somewhere, whimpering as I go.

"You're not doing that move right, Jordan," she told me at cheerleading practice today.

"What?" I put my hands on my hips and stared at her.

Then she demonstrated—or showed off, depending on how you look at it—exactly *how* the move is "supposed" to be done.

"Is that right?" I asked Amber, since she calls the shots.

She nodded.

"Well, fine." Ignoring Shawna, I proceeded to do the move "correctly" for Amber.

"That's better," said Amber.

"Well, a little," said Shawna in her snootiest voice. "But Jordan still needs to work on it."

"It looks okay," said Ashley.

"Yeah, if *okay* is good enough," said Shawna. "But Ms. Brookes says we have to be absolutely perfect if we want to make it into finals at Flair Fair next month. That means we have to be a whole lot better than just *okay*."

Now Flair Fair is the statewide cheerleading competition that Ms. Brookes, our staff adviser, has been talking up for the last few weeks. "This is the best time to really dig in and practice, Jordan," she had told me after I'd privately asked her why we have so many practices between football and basketball season. Dumb me. I'd stupidly thought we'd get a little break.

"That's true," said Betsy Mosler. "*Okay* won't cut it. Like, we could've walked away with first place last year if we'd worked a little harder. JFK wasn't all that great."

"They barely beat us," said Shawna. "That's why we *cannot* settle for Jordan's version of 'okay.'"

I had to literally bite my tongue to keep from responding to that little snipe. *Put on the happy mask.* "Fine," I finally said. "I'll try harder."

"Yeah," said Shawna. "You better. We don't need your inexperience dragging us down this year."

I looked over to Amber now, hoping she might say or do something to give me strength, but she just shrugged and said, "Well, let's get back at it then. I, for one, have to be out of here by five."

And so I really did try harder, but it seemed that every time I turned around, Shawna was finding fault with me again. It wasn't too long before I began to look at the other girls more closely, curious as to whether I was really messing up that badly or not, and that's when I noticed that several others, including Betsy Mosler and Jenny Brighton, weren't doing any better than I was. In fact I think they were actually doing worse. Of course, I didn't dare mention this. I can't afford to risk any more relationships. Having Shawna dogging my case is bad enough without alienating everyone.

Then, to add insult to injury, after I went to the locker room to shower and change, I couldn't find my jeans. Not anywhere. It's like they'd vanished into thin air.

"Anybody seen my jeans?" I asked.

"Having trouble keeping your pants on?" teased Betsy.

I faked a smile. "I'm not the one with that particular problem." I turned to look at Shawna now and couldn't help but notice this little glimmer in her eye like she knew something. "Did you take them?" I asked her point-blank.

"I'm sure!" She looked seriously offended now. "Like I would *steal* your jeans, Jordan. Sheesh, get a life."

"I didn't say you stole them, Shawna, but maybe you just put them—"

"Hey, don't go blaming me just because you can't keep track of your things, Jordan."

I shook my head and, knowing I was getting nowhere, just

pulled on my slightly sweaty practice shorts. "Fine. Whatever." Then I grabbed my stuff and left. But as I walked out to the parking lot, I was seriously fuming. "Can't keep track of your things," I muttered to myself as I furiously searched through my bag for my keys. I'm sure that Shawna meant I couldn't keep track of Timothy that stupid night when she'd seduced him.

That's when I realized my car was still parked in the *other* parking lot, which meant I had to walk two more blocks to get there. Arggh! After nearly freezing my rear end off, I finally reached my car in the nearly deserted parking lot that's right next to the staff lot. Why had I parked here in the first place? But even when I found my car, I realized that I still hadn't found my keys. So, feeling like a total idiot—is sixteen too young to get Alzheimer's?—I threw my bag onto the pavement and knelt down, pawing through the various contents a girl needs throughout the course of a day, in a wild and frantic search for my car keys.

But finally it became painfully clear that they really were *not* there. Like my favorite pair of jeans, which weren't cheap, they had completely and mysteriously disappeared. And it must've been like twenty degrees outside, and I was about to turn into an ice cube in my still-damp shorts that I'm sure were starting to freeze to my buns.

So, out of pure frustration, I first kicked my stupid bag and then my poor car. And to my utter and total surprise and dismay, I actually put a small dent in the innocent front fender. Totally infuriated with everyone, including myself, I cut loose with a whole bunch of four-letter expressions I would normally never use, never have used. But it's like I just needed to get it out.

"*Jordan Ferguson!*" said a woman's voice from behind me. And that's when I turned to see Ms. Brookes only a few feet away and beside her the vice principal, Mr. Myers.

It's at times like this that I can almost believe those stories about these guys in India who just internally combust and explode and disappear into a poof of smoke and ashes—because that's exactly how I felt just then.

"Did we just hear what we thought we heard?" asked Ms. Brookes as she approached me with a very concerned look on her face. Mr. Myers was standing by his car, watching us with what seemed like way too much interest. I was *toast*.

I looked down at the contents of my bag splayed across the parking lot like a mini garage sale and actually considered lying and denying that I'd actually used foul language. Maybe I could make them believe I'd said words that only *sounded* like the profanity I'd just spewed. And even though I've always considered myself an honest person, I suddenly wondered why it should even matter anymore. I mean, why should I care about something as small as telling a lie when I slowly seem to be turning into someone else anyway? But then I reminded myself there were two witnesses— and both of them faculty members.

"I'm so sorry, Ms. Brookes," I confessed, glancing uneasily at Mr. Myers and wondering if I should shout out an apology for him to hear as well. "And I would never talk like that normally, but, you see, I'm just having a really, really bad day. First I lost my jeans and then I lost—"

She held up her hand to stop me. "Jordan, there is no excusable reason to talk like that. Now, you know that you signed the cheer-leader pledge, promising to conduct yourself in a certain manner worthy of a cheerleader." She looked over to where Mr. Myers was still standing, waiting, I'm sure, to see if she handled this correctly. "And as you know, cussing and swearing was something that was clearly listed under item number five on the pledge." She firmly shook her head. "Now even though it may not seem as bad as using drugs or alcohol, it is entirely unacceptable. You girls are supposed to be role models."

"I know." I nodded and attempted to look truly contrite, although the truth was I was still totally steamed. Like, I'm sure, doesn't Ms. Brookes know that Betsy cusses like a sailor half the time? Or that everyone except for me and Jenny Brighton indulges in drinking on a fairly regular basis? The only rule that I don't personally know of being broken by any cheerleaders is the drug use one. And to be perfectly honest, it wouldn't surprise me to find out that Shawna uses something to keep her weight down, because she almost admitted as much to me once back when we were still friends.

"So I'm going to have to put you on probation," she told me with a sad expression. And for a moment I wondered if I might have gotten off if not for Mr. Myers' presence.

"What exactly does that mean?" I asked.

"It means that you are suspended from cheerleading for the next two weeks."

"Okay." I nodded. I could handle this. After all, the first game wasn't until early December, and Flair Fair wasn't until after Christmas. Maybe this wasn't really such a bad consequence. I attempted a meek smile.

"And that means no practicing as well, Jordan."

"What?"

"You aren't allowed to be with the cheerleaders for two weeks."

"You're kidding, right?"

"No, I am not. Perhaps this will be a good reminder to everyone that we really enforce the standards." Satisfied, I'm sure, that she had ruined my life, she turned and smiled at Mr. Myers, who was finally getting into his SUV.

"But, Ms. Brookes," I pleaded with her as he drove away, "that means I won't know the routines for Flair Fair, not to mention basketball season."

"I know. It's a shame too. Somehow the squad will just have to get by without you." And with that she just walked over to her car and drove away.

Now, you'd think that I would've had time to cool off as I walked home from school in the freezing cold wearing my practice shorts, since as fate would have it my cell phone battery was totally dead, but I think I only got madder and madder with each stupid step. I was quickly becoming enraged and felt seriously worried for anyone who crossed my path.

By the time I got home, there was absolutely no reasoning with me. I figured the smart ones would just get out of my way.

"What's wrong?" asked Leah as I stormed in the back door and threw my bag on the floor.

"Life sucks!" I growled as I pushed my way past her.

Fortunately, she had the good sense not to say anything else, because I think I might've done her some serious damage.

"I need a ride to Scouts," yelled Tommy as soon as he spied me going up the stairs.

"Ask someone else!" I snarled at him.

"But Mom and Dad aren't here," he said. "You're supposed to take me."

I turned around and glared at him. "I *cannot* take you to Scouts or anywhere else tonight. *So just forget it!*" Then I went into my room and slammed the door so hard that my mirror actually fell off. I couldn't believe it didn't break since it would only make sense that this day would have been followed by seven long years of bad luck.

Right now my plan is never to emerge from my room again,

because if I do, I am quite certain that I will kill someone—Shawna Frye, to be exact. I have no doubt that she not only stole my boyfriend but also my jeans *and* my car keys. And I seriously wish she were dead.

nine

THANK GOODNESS IT'S FRIDAY, I TOLD MYSELF AS I DROVE TO SCHOOL today. If I could just make it through this day, I would have two blissful days to recover from my increasingly messy life—which is rather ironic, since I totally abhor messes of any kind, particularly when they're related to me.

Of course, the only reason I had a car to drive today was because my dad drove me back over to the school to get mine last night. That was after my little brother called my parents and told them that I was going totally crazy and that they'd better get home before he called up the mental hospital and asked them to take me away.

I'm sure he thought he had good reason to do this since I was basically flipping out in my room, screaming and throwing things and carrying on like a wild woman—and creating more messes, as it turned out. Pretty much out of character. Actually, it wasn't quite as bad as it sounded, although I did break a lamp. But it was an old lamp, and I didn't really care for it anyway.

"It's like I don't know who I am anymore," I had complained as my dad drove me toward school. "My whole life is just totally falling to pieces, and it's like I can't do anything to stop it. It's like it's all just totally out of control."

I'd already told him pretty much the whole ugly story while we pigged out on ice cream at O'Grady's. Okay, I may have left out a few critical things, but a girl's got to have *some* privacy.

"Sometimes you just need to get perspective," he told me as he pulled into the high-school parking lot.

"What do you mean?"

"I know it's hard for you to understand since you're right in the thick of this now, but believe me, this will all pass. What seems huge and impossible to you today will be just a memory before long. You might even laugh about it someday."

I turned around in the seat and stared at him like he had a hairy purple wart growing on the tip of his nose. "*Laugh* about it?"

"You might, someday."

"Yeah, sure." I reached for the door handle now.

"I know this is hard on you, Jordan, but sometimes these hard things have ways of making us stronger, better people."

I rolled my eyes at him, thinking he was starting to sound just like Kara Hendricks. "Well, I don't want to be a stronger or better person, Dad. I just want my old life back."

He smiled. "I know, honey. Maybe you should just do like the Good Book says and try to take it one day at a time."

Well, that sounded manageable, so that's exactly what I decided to do. *Just get through this day,* I told myself as I walked to my first class.

"I hear you're on probation," said Ashley when she spotted me heading toward the English department.

I frowned. "How'd the word get out so fast?"

"Ms. Brookes posted a memo for the cheerleaders."

"Great." I sighed. "Shawna is probably elated."

"What happened?"

I told Ashley the sweetened, condensed version, carefully emphasizing my suspicions that Shawna had stolen both my keys and jeans. And Ashley was appropriately indignant. "That is so unfair," she said as I reached my class.

"Tell me about it." I just shrugged, playing up my role as innocent victim, figuring I'd better milk this for all it's worth since the cheerleaders could get seriously mad at me for getting suspended and messing things up for Flair Fair.

"Well, I'm going to tell the others," she said.

I wanted to hug her and say, "Thank you, thank you!" but instead I continued to play the hopeless fatalist. "It won't change anything."

"Well, it's just *not* fair."

Throughout the day, I got a mixture of sympathy and irritation from the girls. Some—influenced by Shawna, I'm sure—believed my stupidity in the parking lot was going to cost them first place at Flair Fair. Others felt, like Ashley, that the whole scenario was totally unfair. Amber fell somewhere in the middle.

"We all know that everyone breaks the rules *sometimes*," she told me at lunch. "The thing is, you have to be smart about it, Jordan. You don't break the rules on the school grounds, and you never break the rules when Ms. Brookes or any faculty member is in the vicinity."

"Tell me something I don't know," I muttered.

Then, of course, Shawna *had* to show up. "Way to go, Ferguson," she said. It was weird though. She was trying to act all indignant and mad, but it was plain to see, at least to me, that she was totally elated.

"Just chill," said Ashley. "Jordan feels bad enough."

I looked evenly at Shawna now, determined to keep my victim

mask on. "Anytime you'd like to return my car keys and jeans, I'd appreciate it."

"What are you saying?" she asked in a wounded tone. "Are you actually accusing me?"

"If the shoe fits."

She looked around at the other girls, who were all looking at her now. "Well, I can't believe that you really think that I—"

"Give it a rest, Shawna," said Ashley in a bored voice. "We all know you did it."

Shawna's eyes grew wide, almost teary too. What a drama queen!

"Well!" Then she picked up her tray and walked away from the table. And for a moment I thought I had actually won—until I saw her going over to meet Timothy, who had just entered the cafeteria with some of his jock friends. I could only guess what she was saying to him. She was probably telling him that I had personally assaulted her, maybe even threatened her life. After all, Timothy is actually a rather sweet and protective sort of guy when it comes to his girl, or girls—kind of the knight on the white horse. And, naturally, I knew he would feel sorry for her and want to comfort her and help her feel better.

And that is when I got my most brilliant idea yet.

Now if only I can figure out how to execute it without revealing my hand or breaking the law. I don't really want to get pressed with any criminal charges. Especially since I'm already in plenty of trouble as it is.

ten

I WAS SURPRISED TO RUN INTO KARA HENDRICKS AS I WAS LEAVING SCHOOL today, and I hated to brush her off, since she is actually one of the few truly good people in this life, even if she is a bit naive and clueless about some things, like boys, but it seemed I had no choice.

"Sorry. Gotta run," I told her.

"Is everything okay with you?" she asked, concern in her eyes.

I shrugged and dangled my car keys (my spare pair) as in, *hint hint—gotta go now.* "Sure, Kara; everything's fine. Peachy keen."

She frowned. "It doesn't seem fine, Jordan. In fact, it seems like you've really been changing lately."

I smiled like the phony I'm becoming and just shook my head. "Sorry you see it that way, Kara. But really, I've gotta go."

"Well, I'm praying for you, Jordan," she called out after me.

Sheesh, why not tell the whole world? But I couldn't let her get to me right now. I had bigger fish to "frye," like Shawna.

As it turned out, I didn't have to do anything to get Shawna out of the picture for a couple of hours since the cheerleaders were having a special meeting after practice tonight. Ashley had told me their plan was to watch some clandestine videos that Ms. Brookes had just gotten through a friend. Now, talk about breaking the rules. Doesn't it seem just a little unethical that Ms. Brookes had other cheerleading squads secretly videotaped so that we (well, not me since I am excluded while on probation) could study them and possibly increase our chances of taking home a Flair Fair trophy next month? But Ashley said there are no "rules" against such behaviors and that "everybody does it." So who am I to understand such things, being such a social disgrace and all?

But at least their little spy flick would buy me some precious time to attempt, and hopefully carry out, my plan. First of all, I went home for a bit, just to do a little primping. Then I drove back to the parking lot by the gym, where, according to my calculations, Ms. Brookes' film fair would be just starting. More important, Timothy's basketball practice would just be ending, and the boys would be heading for the showers.

I parked near, but not right next to, a certain red Mustang and then, covertly removing an ice pick from my purse just like I was starring in the latest 007 movie, I punctured a tire. Not on the Mustang—good grief, that would be too obvious and might actually get me into serious trouble. And not on Shawna's car either— that plan would surely backfire.

No, I punctured the tire on my very own car and watched in satisfaction as it hissed its way flat. Then, as if to make my cause even more pitiful, it actually started to rain. Maybe God had decided to take my side for a change. To add to the perfect timing, as I stood there getting soggy and just shaking my head in the most dismal fashion, I heard voices coming up from behind me—guy voices, including what I felt certain must be Timothy's.

I knelt down as if to examine my pancake tire, then stood and rummaged through my purse (pretending to look for my phone, which was conveniently not there). "Shoot!" I said loudly, careful not to use any forbidden words and be sentenced to even more probation (or worse, expulsion).

I turned around and, spotting Timothy already looking my direction, ran over to him and did my best impersonation of a damsel in distress.

"I can't believe it," I told him, actually working tears into my eyes. Or was it just the rain?

"What's wrong?" he asked, clearly concerned.

"I've got a flat tire," I told him. "Can you believe it? It's like nothing whatsoever is going right in my life!" I looked up at him with pleading eyes.

"Yeah, I heard you got kicked out of cheerleading too."

"Not exactly kicked out," I said quickly, trying to preserve what little reputation I had left. "I'm just on probation." I attempted to regain my troubled expression again, although I was thinking that stupid Shawna had probably told him and anyone willing to listen that I'd been "kicked off" the squad entirely. Oh, well.

"Want some help?" he offered.

I brightened. "Oh, would you, Timothy?"

"Yeah. Where do you keep the spare in that little clown car?"

I smiled and pointed to the hood. "You still call it that?"

And you can imagine my complete surprise when he pulled out the spare tire only to discover that it too was flat. (I'd taken care of that earlier.)

"Man, that just figures," I told him, shaking my head sadly. "It just goes with the rest of my pitiful little life." I tried to take the floppy spare tire from him now, but he insisted on placing it back in the car himself.

"I'm sorry to have bothered you, Tim," I told him. "Now, if I can just find my cell phone, I'll call someone to come get me." I dug around in my purse for a while, then held it out for him to inspect.

"Am I totally blind? Do you see my cell in there anywhere?" I'd already taken care to conceal the ice pick in a zippered pocket.

"I don't see it either," he said quickly. "But we're getting soaked, Jordan. Why don't you just get in my car and I'll give you a ride."

"But I don't want to trouble—"

He grabbed me by the arm then. "Come on, Jordan. It's no big deal, really."

So, tucked warm and snug in his Mustang, I leaned back into the seat and sighed. "Oh, Timothy, did I ever tell you how much I totally love this car?"

He turned and looked at me in surprise. "Really? You like it? Shawna thinks it smells like gasoline."

I rubbed my hand over the dash. "I think it smells like the good old days." Man, was I hitting it or what?

He smiled. "Yeah, me too."

"We had some great times in here, Tim."

He nodded and started the ignition. "Where do you want to go?"

I smiled in what I hoped was a seductive way and then said, in a lowered voice, "Hey, I think I'd go anywhere you wanted to take me, Timothy."

He laughed. "Is that a come-on, Jordan?"

Now I pretended to pout a little. "I'm sorry, Tim. But you have absolutely no idea how hard it's been on me to lose you."

"Really?" He turned and looked at me like I was putting him on, but to be completely truthful, that was about the most honest thing I'd said so far.

"Cross my heart and hope to die, Tim."

"But you didn't act like it when we broke up," he said, clearly confused. "I didn't think you really cared that much."

"I guess I'm just not that kind of person—to hang on once I

know it's over. I mean, I figured, hey, if you like Shawna more than me, well, what can I do about that?" Now I placed my hand on his thigh. A bold move perhaps, but I felt slightly desperate just then, like this might be my one and only chance and I'd better make good use of it or else just throw in the towel.

Timothy looked pretty surprised but not displeased. In fact, he was smiling.

"Looking back, maybe I handled it all wrong," I said. "What do you think? Did I totally blow it with you, Tim?"

He seemed to consider this as he put the car into gear and started to back up. "We better get out of here, Jordan."

I laughed. "Are you worried someone will see us together?"

"I'm not sure."

It wasn't long before we were parked in a fairly secluded parking lot on the far side of the city park. And with the rain pouring down and the windows getting fogged by our heated breath, we kissed with a passion that was unlike anything I'd ever felt before. It was almost savage the way we were grabbing for each other. And then we managed to crawl, somewhat awkwardly, into the backseat, where there was only a little more room but at least no gear shift lodged between us.

This is going to be it, I told myself with real determination. *I am going to do IT. I am going to win this guy back even if it means I have to give in completely. I'm going to win him back, and then he'll be mine—all mine!* The thought both thrilled and terrified me.

And in that same moment, we heard a loud thumping noise on the roof of the car, and it didn't seem to be the rain. Timothy rolled down the window to see his own father, a very damp and somewhat disturbed-looking Mr. Lawrence, peering into the car with obvious curiosity.

"What is going on here?" he asked abruptly, and then seeing me, cowering behind Tim, his brows lifted as if he knew exactly what was going on. *"Timothy?"*

"I—uh—I—"

"I thought something was wrong with your car," said Mr. Lawrence quickly, and it was clear to see that the poor man was uncomfortable by his discovery. "I thought maybe you'd broken down."

"Nothing's wrong, Dad." Timothy's voice was slightly irritated.

"Well, I was on my way home from work and I just happened to notice your car as I drove on the overpass." He cleared his throat. "Couldn't imagine why you'd be out here in the middle of the rain like this."

"Jordan had a flat tire," said Timothy. As if *that* explained everything. "I was just helping her."

Mr. Lawrence shook his head. "That's not how you fix a tire, son."

"We're just leaving, Dad." Timothy got out of the car and went around to the front door as I climbed back into the passenger seat, feeling pretty trampy. But here's what's really weird about this whole scenario: I also felt relieved. *Hugely relieved.* So much so that I actually had to hide the grin that might have destroyed everything. Instead, I hunched down and folded my arms across my chest and acted as if I'd just been denied the greatest opportunity of my entire life.

Timothy got inside the car and exhaled loudly as he watched his dad drive away. Then he punched the steering wheel and cussed.

"Yeah, it just figures," I said, still hunched over and looking seriously disgruntled.

"Huh?"

"Well, *nothing* is going right for me anymore." I made this groaning sound. "It's just not fair, Tim. Since you left me, my life has just gone from bad to worse to totally messed up and hopeless. I should be wearing a big *L* on my head for 'loser.'"

He turned around and patted my head. "I think you're being too hard on yourself, Jordie."

I smiled at him. Now usually I hate to be called Jordie, but it sounded kind of sweet coming from him.

"I think we better head out," he said.

"Yeah, I guess."

So he started his car and I dug around in my purse until I found some tissues and helped him clean the fog off the front windows. "Got pretty steamy in here," I said in a slightly suggestive tone.

"That's for sure."

"I guess you should probably take me home now," I told him, sounding disappointed again. "I'll need to get some help getting my tire fixed and everything."

"I'd help you," he said, "but I, well, I was supposed to see Shawna tonight."

I nodded. "So, are you going to tell her about what happened today?"

He sighed. "I don't know."

"Well, I'm sure not going to pressure you, Timothy. I like you way too much to pull something stupid like that. But I will tell you this much. I'm not one of those girls who can be kept secretly on the side, if you know what I mean. I'm a one-guy kind of girl, and I want a one-girl kind of guy. You know?"

"I know."

When we reached my house, I leaned over and kissed him. First on the cheek, then I pulled his face toward me and planted a big long kiss on his mouth. My best shot.

It seemed to be working too, because when I pulled away and opened my eyes to look at him, it was plain to see he was slightly stunned. I actually thought I saw stars in those dark brown eyes.

"See you," I said lightly as I opened the door and let myself out.

eleven

"Was that who I thought it was?" asked my dad when I came in the house. He set his newspaper aside and seemed to be studying me with father-like curiosity.

I nodded. "I guess you were right, Dad. My life isn't as bad as I thought after all."

He got this strange expression just then, kind of a combination of relief mixed with serious concern.

"By the way, I got a flat tire and the spare was flat too."

He narrowed his eyes. "The *spare* tire was flat?"

"Yeah, pretty weird, huh?"

"I'll say." He frowned. "I remember checking it when we got your car."

I shrugged. "These things happen."

It was almost seven o'clock by the time we got a new spare onto my car. He and the tire guy were both curious as to how both of my tires had suffered similar puncture wounds.

"I think someone's out to get me," I told them with an absolutely serious expression. "My keys got stolen and who knows what's going on?" Okay, it did bother me that I have suddenly turned into this big fat liar. But desperate times call for desperate measures. And as Amber has told me a number of times, all is fair . . .

Anyway, after the repaired tire was securely on my car, I told my dad to go ahead and take off.

"I can put this stuff away," I told him after he gave the last bolt a final crank and stood up.

"Well, at least you know how to change a tire now," he told me as he wiped his hands on his handkerchief.

"Thanks, Dad. I guess it's like you said last night."

He looked slightly hopeful. "What's that?"

"You know, that whole spiel about tough times making you stronger."

He smiled. "See?"

"But, really, go ahead and go. I'll be fine." I took the wrench from him. "Besides, I need to stick around and talk to Ashley for a minute."

"What's Ashley doing here still?" He glanced at his watch. "It's almost seven."

I still hadn't told my parents about my probation problem. I know I'll have to explain it eventually. But it's like I've got enough crud to deal with right now without having them on my case about using foul language too.

"The cheerleaders were supposed to watch these videotapes," I told him, "but when I realized my tire was flat I thought I'd better come get you so we could get it fixed before it got too late." I wasn't sure if he was buying this or not. "I didn't want to have to interrupt your evening again tonight."

"Well, thanks for that." He shook his head. "Don't be out late, Jordan. Leah's home alone tonight since Tommy is spending the night at Slater's house."

"I won't be late," I assured him. "Tell Leah she can call me on my cell if she needs to. And you guys have a good time tonight."

He frowned. "We will. You're going to be okay, aren't you?"

I smiled my most assuring smile. "I've never been better, Dad. Really, don't worry about me."

Then I pulled my cell phone out of the glove box, where I'd conveniently stowed it during my damsel-in-distress routine, and held it up. "I'm only a phone call away."

The rain had stopped now, and the pavement in the parking lot glistened beneath the bright streetlights like a sheet of silver as my dad pulled away. I didn't bother putting anything away just yet. I wanted to be sure that the flat tire and jack were still lying next to my car.

"Jordan," called Ashley as the cheerleaders poured into the parking lot. "What are you doing here?" Then she looked down at the tire and stuff. "What's wrong?"

Soon the cheerleaders were all gathered around me. Funny how people get so curious when something appears to be wrong.

"Oh, no big deal," I assured them. "I just had a flat tire this afternoon."

"But why are you here so late?" asked Amber.

"Well, it's a long story. Basically, my spare tire was flat too, so Timothy was sweet enough to give me a ride and then we got sort of sidetracked." I laughed as if I had some secret little joke. "And, anyway, all's well that ends well. Right?" I looked directly at Shawna now and grinned victoriously.

"Oh, I'm sure," she said, as if I'd made up the whole story.

I turned and smiled at the other girls. "So, how were the cheer-leading espionage movies?"

"Totally lame," said Ashley. "Waste of time."

"If that little story is true," said Shawna, grabbing me by the arm with a grip that actually pinched a little, "then where is he now?"

"Huh?" I looked at her like I didn't know what she meant. "Who?"

"Timothy, stupid. Where is he now?"

"Well, after he dropped me off, he told me he was supposed to see you tonight." I shrugged. "I'm guessing he went home to brace himself for the little hissy fit you'll be throwing before the night is over."

Naturally, she looked enraged. Without saying another word, she stomped over to her Toyota.

"Shut *up!*" said Ashley as she slapped me on the back. "Is this for real? Are you and Timothy really back together again?"

"We were this afternoon," I said lightly. "I guess we'll have to see what happens next."

"Shawna looks pretty ticked," said Jenny as we all watched her tear out of the parking lot. I was surprised she didn't try to smack the big mud puddle next to me and drench me, but then she would've gotten the other girls wet too. Bad style.

"Duh," said Betsy. "Wouldn't you be?"

"Well, here we go again," said Amber, not a bit amused.

Yeah, here we go again. And what a ride it's gonna be this time, now that I know the "real rules," as in "All is fair in love and war."

twelve

I WASN'T SURE WHAT TO DO AFTER I LEFT THE SCHOOL THAT NIGHT. I didn't really want to go home and hang with my little sister on a Friday night. I mean, how lame is that? And Ashley was going out with Brett, so I couldn't exactly hang with her. Even so, I was feeling totally jazzed for her. Way to go, Ash!

So that's when I knew I had to go cruising. I've decided not to call it *stalking* anymore. That is way too demeaning. No, I was going cruising. Big deal if I happened to *cruise* by Timothy's house. And I wasn't all that surprised that his car wasn't there. Then I happened to go cruising by Shawna's house and, bingo, the red Mustang was parked right in front. Hopefully, it would only be parked there briefly. I imagined Timothy, having learned from the mess he made of things last time, politely telling Shawna that it was over. That's a scene I would pay big money to witness. Just the same, I didn't want to take any chances at being spotted, so I kept my phone turned on and continued cruising.

It's hard to find much to do in our town when it's not a game night and there's not a party going on. And after what happened to Ashley, I don't know if anyone's real excited about throwing a party these days. Besides, with Thanksgiving next week, I suppose most parents are staying close to home right now.

But after cruising for about thirty minutes, I decided to swing by Shawna's again, just to check and see. And to my pleasant surprise, the red Mustang was gone. But when I went by Timothy's, it wasn't there either. So naturally, I decided to check at what has rapidly become the most popular hangout, a new coffee shop called Jitters Java. And, bingo again, there was the red Mustang. Fortunately, Jitters is almost all windows, and it was easy to peer inside as I slowly cruised by. But I didn't like what I saw: There, at a corner table, sat Timothy and Shawna. I couldn't tell by their expressions whether they were having a good time, or if Timothy possibly had brought her to a public place to make his little announcement. (Less chance of an enraged hissy fit with witnesses around.)

I knew I couldn't just lay low. I wanted to go in. Problem was, I didn't want to go in alone. And, being Friday, I figured my chances of scaring up a friend were fairly minimal—unless Kara happened to be home.

I dialed her number as I drove toward her apartment complex. Although she's never seen it this way, I think she's totally lucky to live so close to school and town. She can get anywhere within a couple of minutes. Of course, she thinks I'm the lucky one because I live in a full-sized house out in the suburbs. I guess the grass really is always greener on the other side.

Fortunately for me, she answered the phone.

"Hi, Kara," I said in a slightly dismal voice, hoping I could reel her in with no resistance.

"What's wrong?"

"Nothing much. I guess I just wanted to talk. I was thinking about what you said today, you know, about how I've changed and all, and I just wanted to hear what you're thinking. Do you want to get a cup of coffee?"

To my relief, she was game. But to my dismay, when I picked her up, she was *not* alone. Edgar the Dweeb was with her. Now, I'm sure he's a perfectly nice guy. Kara certainly seems to think so. But despite his recent makeover, which actually helped some, everyone at school (well, my friends anyway) thinks Edgar Peebles is a total nerd.

Still, I bit my tongue as they climbed in my car. What could I say? Besides, I was on a mission. Within minutes we had parked across the street and were walking past a certain red car and going into Jitters Java.

"Have you guys been here yet?" I asked them, glancing over my shoulder to see if my entrance was being noticed by anyone in particular. Fortunately, the place was fairly crowded and Tim wasn't looking. A relief since I was now risking being seen with not only Kara but her nerdy friend as well.

"We've been here a couple of times," Kara told me.

"Really?" Now, I don't know why this surprised me, but I guess I tend to think that people like Kara and Edgar have no life.

"Yeah, Edgar is teaching me to appreciate coffee," she said. "Well, as long as it has something sweet in it, like chocolate."

"Yeah," added Edgar. "We'll work you up to the really good stuff like espresso later."

After we ordered, the three of us went and sat down on the other side of the room. I made sure that I took the chair with a perfect view of a certain couple, with Kara and Edgar on the other side. Timothy's back was to me now, but I figured Shawna would see me if she ever looked my direction.

"Hello?" said Kara impatiently. "Earth to Jordan. Can you read me?"

"Huh?" I kind of blinked. "Sorry."

"So, you're still carrying a torch for old Timothy Lawrence?" said Edgar as if he knew everything.

"Carrying a torch?" I frowned at him. "Where do you *get* this stuff?"

Kara rolled her eyes at me as she took a sip of her café mocha. "So is that why we're here then, Jordan?"

"No." I shook my head for added emphasis. "I just wanted to talk to you." I glanced uncomfortably at Edgar. I hadn't really wanted to include him in this. "What you said today really bugged me, Kara." Actually, that was true.

"Well, I *do* think you've changed, Jordan. And I don't want to offend you, but it's not an improvement."

"Thanks."

Edgar gently nudged Kara with his elbow.

"Sorry," she said, although I wasn't sure if she was talking to me or to him. "Sometimes the truth hurts."

"And I suppose you think it's only fair that you should be the one to do the hurting this time?" I asked.

"This time?"

"Oh, I know that I hurt you, Kara. I've told you I'm sorry dozens of—"

"That doesn't have anything to do with this, Jordan."

"Yeah, sure." I was feeling slightly uncomfortable that Edgar was witnessing this little scene, but then I wondered why I should care.

"It doesn't," she insisted. "The only reason I even said anything is because I really care about you."

"And you can honestly tell me you wouldn't get a little bit of pleasure out of hurting me, Kara?"

"No, Jordan. I just wish I could say something tonight to help you see that you're worth more than this."

"More than what?"

"Oh, you know. Playing your stupid games, chasing after some guy who just wants to use you and then lose you."

"Kara," said Edgar in a soft voice. "You don't really know that."

I nodded, thinking maybe this Edgar guy wasn't such a loser after all. "Yeah," I said. "You don't really know that."

She shook her head. "No, he's just trying not to be judgmental. But I'm not as highly evolved a Christian as Edgar. And I think Timothy Lawrence is only after one thing when it comes to you."

"You don't know a thing about it." I heard my voice increase in volume, but fortunately the room was crowded and the music was loud. No one except Kara and Edgar even noticed. I tried not to stare at the couple in the far corner whose heads were now tilted toward each other in an intimate way, as if they were enjoying some special secret. I was starting to feel sick to my stomach.

"Jordan?" Kara patted me on the arm to get my attention. "What is wrong with you anyway? It's like you've totally checked out."

"Sorry." I turned my attention back to them.

"Are you okay?" asked Edgar with what seemed genuine concern.

"I don't know."

"Really, Jordan," said Kara. "What's going on with you? Are you seriously pining away for that stupid jock?"

"Kara," said Edgar in a warning voice. "You're doing it again."

"Sorry." She shook her head. "I just feel protective of Jordan."

This was somewhat touching, but I still felt sick.

"Okay, let me rephrase that. Jordan," she said again, "do you still think you love Timothy Lawrence?"

At first I didn't answer, and then finally I mumbled a barely audible, "Maybe." I looked down at my untouched espresso, feeling seriously embarrassed by the fact that (1) I was the short end of a love triangle, and (2) I had just confessed this to a couple of losers.

"Well, he's not worth it, Jordan."

"Kara," said Edgar with a slightly exasperated sigh, as if he were getting weary of playing Christian cop with her.

"Well, he's *not*, Edgar. He's just using Jordan."

"How would you even know?" I demanded.

She just shrugged at my jab, but I could tell by her eyes she was hurt.

"Sorry," I muttered.

"It's okay. I can see that you're hurting right now and maybe you think it'll make you feel better to hurt someone else too."

I nodded. "Yeah, maybe it would make me feel better to hurt someone. Like, I'd give anything to be able to tear Shawna's freaking bleached hair out by the roots."

Kara's eyes widened, but Edgar actually laughed. Then Kara nodded in triumph, as if I'd just totally made her point for her. "See," she said to Edgar. "That's just what I mean. She really *has* changed." Then she turned back to me. "Jordan, listen to yourself. You've gotten hard, you're becoming increasingly shallow, and now you're plotting violent revenge."

"Give me a break," I said, although I knew she wasn't too far off the mark.

"This isn't the Jordan I used to know," she said to Edgar as if I were totally invisible. "And if you ask me, it's pretty sad."

"I can't believe I wanted to talk to you about this." I looked at both of them now, really looked at them. I was sizing them up in the same way that my cheerleading friends would size up anyone who crossed their path in the wrong way. "Speaking of changing, Kara, you've changed too. And in my opinion, it's *not* for the better either. Like how about the way you dress, for instance? You used to be semi-cool. But what's this new look you're going for these days? 'Art freak' maybe, so you'll fit in better? Really, what's with the baggy overalls and stained T-shirt? Or are you just basically fashion-challenged now that I'm not telling you what to wear anymore? And have you noticed that you hang with a bunch of geeks?" I nodded toward Edgar now as if to include him in my insults since I was on such a roll. It did catch my attention that he seemed to be taking my crud pretty well, but I could see that I'd really hurt Kara, and I must admit that it bothered me some. But then, misery loves company and it seemed that Kara Hendricks and Edgar Peebles were the only company I was going to get tonight, because I looked up just in time to see Timothy and Shawna leaving. He had his hand on her back as he opened the door for her, and she was smiling as if everything in her world was perfectly fine. And that's when I wanted to run into the bathroom and hurl.

By the time I turned back to look at Kara, she was halfway across the room, with Edgar just a step behind her. It seemed everyone was leaving me behind.

Seriously, that's when I knew I was a loser times two.

thirteen

I SPENT THE ENTIRE WEEKEND IN MY ROOM. CALL IT A PITY PARTY, A REALITY check, or just plain hopelessness, but I did not want to see or talk to anyone.

"What's wrong?" my mom asked me for like the millionth time on Sunday night.

"I just want to be alone," I told her in a calm voice. Same thing I'd said over and over every time whichever designated family member knocked on my door. It's like they assumed it was their responsibility to keep checking on me. What, did they think I might, like, do myself in? Actually, I'd already considered it, but being a chicken, basically, I didn't think I would attempt anything crazy. At least not right then.

The upside of all this isolation was that my room was completely tidy. I'm sure a shrink would say that my obsessive-compulsive side was taking over, trying to bring order to at least one area of my life since the rest of it was totally nuts. And I suppose that might be true. It did feel good to have just a teeny bit of control. Unfortunately, that's where it ended. Tomorrow I'd be going back to school and subjected to utter social chaos. And I didn't even have a plan this time.

I got out my notebook and told myself I was going to do my

homework, but soon I was doodling and daydreaming of various ways I could seriously injure Shawna.

First I considered leaving her an anonymous treat laced with laxatives. Too grade school. Then I considered cutting some crucial seam threads in her cheerleading uniform right before the pep assembly. I imagined the student body laughing as her skirt fell off. Not bad—but not bad enough either. Then I imagined sneaking some kind of toxic powder into her compact so that she would break out into ugly red hives that look just like zits. Too middle school. Then I simply imagined things like keying her "perfect" car or ice-picking all four of her tires. Too illegal. Speaking of illegal, maybe I should have just hired a hit man and had her knocked off. *Too psycho.*

Then I began to think that maybe Kara was right. Maybe I was changing—or just totally losing it. And to my surprise, before I could talk myself out of it, I actually called her up.

"I'm sorry, Kara," I said right off the bat. "I said some totally stupid and mean things to you guys on Friday night. And, really, I'm sorry." I prepared for her to hang up on me, since she did that to me a couple of times after I quit being her best friend a couple of months ago.

"I forgive you," she said in an even-keeled voice.

"You do?" I was totally stunned. "Seriously, you can forgive me just like that?"

"Only because of Jesus."

Oh, no.

"So, how are you doing?" she asked, and I assumed that meant I'd escaped a sermon.

"Not so great."

"Uh-huh."

"Yeah. In fact I've been barricaded in my room all weekend. I'm sure my parents are about ready to call up the Arlington Clinic and see if they have an available bed for me."

She laughed, but not unkindly. "What's going on?"

"I guess I'm depressed."

"Man," she sighed. "It's hard to imagine the forever optimistic and unflappable Jordan Ferguson actually getting depressed. This sounds serious."

"It is. I even wondered how it would feel to do myself in."

Kara was silent for a minute. "Seriously?"

"Yeah. But don't worry. I'm way too much of a coward to really do anything. I mean, there isn't even a gun in the house, and I'm not brave enough to, like, go leap from the top of the Harcourt Insurance building. Even if I took pills, I figure I'd probably just end up at the hospital having my stomach pumped like Leslie Cox back in middle school. Remember her? She was so humiliated that she had to transfer to another school."

"I didn't know that was why she transferred."

"Of course it was. Anyway, I just couldn't take that kind of embarrassment right now. My life is bad enough as it is."

"Is this still about Timothy?"

"And Shawna. Don't forget Shawna."

"So, do you plan to just let this jealousy eat away at you forever, Jordan? Is it your life's ambition to turn into some embittered old woman who never got over her broken heart?"

I wanted to yell at her for that, to say, "What would you know about broken hearts anyway?" But somehow I managed to control myself.

"You want to know what I really think?" she asked after my brief period of controlled silence.

"Do I have a choice, Kara?"

"Hey, you're the one who called *me*."

"Fine. What do you *really* think?"

"I think you're searching for God in all the wrong places."

"Huh?" I wasn't even searching for God. What was she talking about?

"Really. I didn't want to preach at you, Jordan. Edgar says I do it way too much anyway. But the truth is, I think that your recent obsession with Timothy *and* Shawna is really just a placebo for God."

"I still have no idea what you're talking about." When had Kara gotten so deep into her religion that I couldn't even figure out what she was saying anymore? Sheesh, it'd only been a few months since we'd been best friends. It really made me wonder who was doing most of the changing here. "A placebo for God?" I finally said. *"Puh-leeze.* Give me a break, Kara."

"Okay, then can I ask you a question?"

"Sure, why not?"

"Are you happy?"

"Am I happy?" I felt a tightness in my throat just then. Crud, I was the furthest thing from happy at that moment. If happy were Mercury, I'd have been living on Neptune.

"Yeah, Jordan. You made cheerleader, just like you wanted. You got a bunch of new popular friends, just like you wanted. You even dated the guy you've had a crush on for, like, forever, just like you wanted. So tell me, are you happy?"

"Well, not at the moment. But that's only because—"

"Did you ever stop to think that maybe those things aren't really what you wanted after all?" she asked. "Did you ever realize that those things aren't really making you happy?"

"Hey, there's a lot more to it than *that*, Kara." And then for no good reason—other than my pathetic, desperate need to talk—I told her about my probation from cheerleading, and how Ashley was probably my closest friend but even *she* didn't really have time for me now that she was dating Brett Hawkins. I also told her about flattening my own tires and my willingness to have sex with Timothy.

"Really?" she asked in an incredulous tone that made me realize I had told her too much.

"Yeah, and I can't believe I'm telling you all this. I feel like I'm at confession or something."

"You're not even Catholic."

"Duh. But how did you worm all this out of me?"

"Maybe it's because we're still friends, Jordan."

"Well, please don't tell anyone what I said." I forced a laugh. "Not that your nerdy friends would care. But they might."

She cleared her throat. "I'd appreciate it if you didn't call my friends nerdy. Okay?"

"Yeah, whatever."

"Or geeky or dweeby or even stupid. Okay?"

"Fine."

"But really, Jordan, you would've had sex with Timothy just to get him back?"

"And to get back at Shawna."

"Uh-huh." I could tell by the way she said "uh-huh" that she was more like going *"Hmmm."*

"Yeah?"

"Well, it is kind of interesting, don't you think?"

"What?" I demanded.

"You know. That your reason for having sex for the first time—

I assume you're still a virgin—that you would give it up simply because of jealousy."

"I am still a virgin," I snapped. "And it's not about jealousy. You just don't understand anything, Kara. I happen to really, really care about Timothy—a lot! I think that I'm actually in love with him."

"Or obsessed with him. Haven't you ever seen that old movie *Fatal Attraction*?"

"Get real, Kara."

"Okay, okay. But think about *this*, Jordan."

"What?"

"Think about what all *this* is costing you."

"Costing me? What do you mean?"

"I mean, like your tires, for instance. Two tires couldn't have been cheap."

"My dad said I needed new tires anyway."

"Okay, what about your probation? You worked really hard to get picked. It seems a pretty high price to pay—"

"But that was Shawna's fault. She took my keys and—"

"But that never would've happened if you hadn't gotten stuck in a love triangle."

"So, what are you suggesting?"

"Just that you need God more than you need a guy."

I actually laughed at that. "Yeah, whatever."

"Hey, I'm curious about something, Jordan."

"What's that?"

"Well, what time was it when Timothy's dad made his unexpected appearance at just the right moment?"

"You mean the *wrong* moment."

"Whatever."

"I don't know. I'm guessing it was about five thirty."

Well, for whatever reason this just cracked Kara up. She just laughed and laughed like it was the funniest thing she'd heard in ages. This just goes to show how much that girl needs to get a life!

"What's the deal?" I finally asked, irritated to be left out of this joke.

"Oh, nothing." She snickered in the most obnoxious way. "It just so happens that I was really, really praying for you around that exact same time."

"Thanks a lot." I let the sarcasm drip.

"You're very welcome."

"I can't figure you out, Kara."

"Huh?"

"I'm not sure whether you're trying to play my confessor father, saintly friend, or Dr. Bill."

She laughed again. "Maybe all of the above."

After I hung up, I realized that although I'd spilled my guts to her, telling her almost every sordid little detail and way more than I've told anyone, I had still held back on one particular thing: I never told her how relieved I had been when Timothy's dad showed up that afternoon. Maybe it's because I don't totally understand that one myself.

But to be perfectly honest, I don't really want to think about it right now either.

fourteen

I SOMEHOW MADE IT THROUGH THE LAST THREE DAYS WITHOUT PHYSICALLY assaulting Shawna Frye. Once again, I put on my happy mask and actually managed to convince almost everyone that I have moved on. Of course, Kara is on to me, and she gives me this knowing look every time I see her, which fortunately isn't often. Still, I have to wonder what's with that girl anyway.

But underneath my sleek and perfect I-am-just-fine-thank-you-very-much veneer, I feel like I am slowly decaying. It's like this jealousy crud is literally eating me alive. I keep thinking—okay, *obsessing*—about Shawna and Timothy. And it's like I can't stop. Even though I try to be very covert about it, it's like I'm always on the lookout for them. It's like I enjoy the pain of catching them holding hands, embracing, whatever. What is wrong with me?

Thankfully, it's Thanksgiving, which means a shortened school week. I'm actually looking forward to seeing my older sister, Abbie, when she comes home from college. It's kind of weird since we used to constantly fight over the bathroom that we shared, but suddenly I can't wait to see her. For all I care, she can have the bathroom totally to herself. I just need someone to talk to before I crumble. I need someone with a better perspective than, say, Kara, who seems to have only one perspective. I need someone *mature*. I never had a chance to tell Abbie about Timothy, to show her his picture and tell her why I'm so attracted to him and why I can't seem to let go. Somehow I think she'd understand. I think she'd have some answers.

And in Timothy's defense, although I'm not entirely sure why I'd want to defend him just now, he did send me an email last weekend. We used to email each other a lot during the short time we were going out. His notes were actually rather romantic, and for a guy, he writes a pretty good line. But in this particular email, which wasn't the least bit romantic, he basically told me that what happened with us on Friday had been a mistake. Of course, he told me that he was very sorry and then assured me it wouldn't happen again. End of story. Sheesh.

It hasn't helped anything that Shawna is so smug and full of herself these days. Thank goodness I didn't have to go to cheerleading practice this week. It's bad enough to have to sit through lunch, listening to her prattling on about Tim this and Tim that. (Despite my misery, I still make myself sit with my friends in order to hold what social position, low as it is, I still have.) But I'm actually beginning to wonder if it's really worth it. I seriously think I may be getting an ulcer. Even so, I sit next to Ashley and do my best to smile and laugh and act totally normal. And then today, Shawna had to go and say something to me about the Flair Fair routines.

"I don't know how you're *ever* going to catch up, Jordan." She said this in what I'm sure was supposed to sound like a very sympathetic tone.

"Yeah," agreed Betsy. "The routines are pretty hard."

"Maybe you should just call it quits," suggested Shawna kindly. "They're having tryouts for the basketball dance team today. You might be able to make that."

"You mean the Dog Squad," said Betsy, and everyone laughed loudly. The cheerleaders, among others, get a kick out of calling the dance team the Dog Squad. There are two dance teams every year, one for football and one for basketball, and both teams have twenty girls, which actually gives forty girls a chance at participating. But everyone knows that only the cheerleading rejects and major losers ever try out for the Dog Squad. And I suppose I have to agree with popular opinion, since I'd rather be seen picking my nose than dancing with the Dog Squad.

"Maybe I can help you with the routines," suggested Ashley as we were leaving the lunch table. Naturally, she said this in a lowered voice since this could get her into big trouble if Ms. Brookes found out.

I tried to register genuine enthusiasm, but really I just felt like smacking someone right then. Mostly Shawna. "Sure, Ashley," I said with a pasted-on smile. "That'd be great. Do you really have time?"

"Yeah, this weekend is good for me. Not during the day though since I have to work at the mall. Which reminds me, my mom said she'd like to hire you during the Christmas rush. You still interested?"

"Sure."

"Well, why don't we plan on Saturday night then, unless you have a big date." She smiled in a teasing way.

"Yeah, right." I rolled my eyes. "But what about you? Aren't you and Brett going—?"

"He's going to be at the shooting clinic over at the university all weekend."

"Great, then I'll plan on Saturday."

"And you can talk to my mom about the job too."

"Okay."

So, all in all, I guess my life isn't totally hopeless. But I just don't get why it has to be so difficult most of the time. Like, what did I do to deserve this? I especially have to wonder about this at times like tonight, when the stuff finally hit the fan with my parents.

"Why didn't you tell us you were on probation, Jordan?" my mom demanded as I stopped in the kitchen to help her put away about twenty bags of groceries. So much for trying to be nice!

"How'd you hear about that?" I asked.

"I saw Jenny's mom at the store." She sat down a heavy bag and then peered at me curiously.

"Oh." I'd sort of forgotten that Jenny's mom is not only a friend of my mom but that she also has a very big mouth. "I was going to tell you."

"When?"

"I've been busy."

"Doing what?" My mom flopped the turkey onto the counter and then turned around to really study me. "It's obvious that you haven't been doing your homework, Jordan."

"Huh?"

"Your midterm grades."

"Oh, yeah."

She softened. "Really, Jordan, what's going on with you?"

"It's been hard, Mom."

"Is this about Timothy?"

I shrugged and then turned around to put the potatoes in the bin, obviously stalling, as I carefully unloaded them one by one when I could've easily just dumped the entire bag.

"Jordan, you can talk to me," she urged. "I remember what it felt like to be in high school."

I stood up and studied her now. "Really?"

"Yeah, of course."

I shook my head. "But you and I aren't anything alike, Mom."

"Oh, I didn't go for things like cheerleading. And in all fairness it was considered kind of stupid and shallow back in the early seventies. I was more into art and social causes. Did I ever tell you about the time we staged a war protest at—?"

"Yeah, Mom, you told me."

"Oh."

"That's what I mean. We're just different, Mom. Sometimes I think Kara should've been your daughter instead of me."

She smiled. "How is Kara anyway? I saw her a few weeks ago and she told me that she's really getting into art this year."

"Yeah. Art and religion."

She smiled even bigger. "Well, good for her."

I rolled my eyes. "I think I'll go do my homework, Mom."

"That sounds like a good idea."

And so I went to my room, but instead of doing my homework, I went online and checked to see if I had any email. Of course, the only new pieces were spam. "You've won a free vacation!" Yeah, I wish. And "Get out of debt for only $19.99." People who fall for that one should be locked up in the debtors' prison for good.

Then I scrolled down to where I've saved every one of Timothy's emails to me. And, in the mood to torture myself, I began to read them, one by one. Before long I was crying, and then I finally came to the last email. I read it again, more carefully this time, and suddenly I thought it just didn't sound quite right. Something about what he'd written to me about being sorry about last Friday just didn't sound like it was really from the heart. I even wondered if perhaps he'd written it just to pacify Shawna. I could imagine her standing there, looking over his shoulder, smiling smugly as she watched him literally writing me off.

But now I realized that my choice to totally ignore it—I hadn't responded to it at all—might've been a complete mistake. At the time, I'd been frustrated and didn't want to appear like I was trying too hard, especially after that little spiel I'd given him about wanting a one-girl kind of guy. But for some reason I thought maybe it was time to respond now.

"Hey, Tim," I typed out. "Sorry to be so slow getting back to you, but that's life, eh? Thanks for the email. And, hey, don't worry. I think I'm ready to move on now anyway. We had a lot of fun together and I'll always remember the good times. Have a good life. Love, Jordie."

Then I hit send. Now the problem with email is that once you send it, it's gone. And in the next instant, I wished I hadn't bothered. I mean, what was the purpose of this lame attempt to get his attention again? I might've written "I'm moving on" in my email, but it seemed pretty obvious, at least to me, that I was still stuck on the guy if I was still sending him email. But who knew? Maybe this was actually a step in my recovery.

I stared at the pile of books that I actually brought home with me today, thinking I could really knock out a couple of homework projects during the four-day weekend. But instead of opening my history book, I opened my latest issue of *Glamour* and totally lost myself in the fickle world of fashion. Ah, relief.

Of course, I did interrupt myself periodically to go and check my email, just in case Timothy responded—which he didn't. I am truly pathetic.

fifteen

THANKSGIVING WAS A LITTLE DISAPPOINTING. WE HAD A HOUSEFUL OF relatives, and that was okay, but Abbie only stuck around for a short while before she went to hang with her old high-school friends. Not that I blame her. I'd probably do the same thing under the same circumstances. But then she took off early on Friday to go to the mountains with some of her new college friends. Okay, what can I say? Except that, once again, I feel jealous. Sheesh, I really need to get a life.

But then on Saturday, I got a nice surprise. An email from Timothy! And not just a thanks-for-the-note kind of email either. No, it seemed that he was seriously rethinking the whole Shawna thing. Apparently they'd had a fight and he was getting fed up with her stupid games. He actually wanted me to drive over to the university where they were having their shooting clinic so we could *talk*.

"Meet me at the Starbucks on Oak Street at eight o'clock," he wrote. "I think we can figure out a way to get back together for good. Love, Tim."

I couldn't believe it. It seemed my life might finally be turning around. And this time, I didn't even have to do the manipulating. Timothy had come back to me on his own free accord.

"I'm not going to be able to make it tonight," I told Ashley on the phone.

"Why not?" I could hear the irritation in her voice, and suddenly I knew I couldn't tell her it was to drive an hour and a half just to meet Timothy for coffee. I didn't think she'd get it—especially since her theme song to me is "Just move on," and so far I'd managed to convince her that I had. Why mess things up now?

"It's a family emergency," I told her. "My parents have to leave town and I've got to babysit Leah and Tommy." I felt a dryness in my mouth. Lying really doesn't agree with me.

"You can bring them over here," said Ashley. "We can plug them into a video or something. My mom has the whole moronic Disney collection."

"I can't do that," I told her. "Everyone's pretty upset and my parents really want me to stay home and keep things calm for them."

"Wow, what happened anyway?"

I thought for a moment. "It's my sister Abbie. She went to the mountains with some friends and something happened. We don't even know for sure what."

"Man, that's too bad. Well, let me know if she's okay, Jordan. That's a bummer."

"I know. But hopefully it'll all sort out. Maybe we can practice tomorrow."

"I have to work again. But maybe tomorrow night. Although Brett will be home by then and I hate to miss seeing him. I'll let you know, okay?"

"Okay."

"And, really, I'm sorry about your sister and everything. I hope she's okay."

"Yeah, thanks." I hung up and felt slimy as toilet-bowl scum. I mean, what on earth was wrong with me? How had I turned into such a total liar?

The only thing that was perfectly clear to me was that love can make you do strange things.

Well, as long as I was getting myself in deeper and deeper, I decided to lie to my parents as well. For one thing, I knew they wouldn't approve of me driving so far at night. And to meet a guy? Well, I could just forget about that. So I went along with my previous plan and told my mom that I was going to Ashley's to learn the new routines and talk to her mom about a job.

"That's great, Jordan," said my mom. "I'm glad to see you're getting back on track."

I smiled my little happy smile and nodded. "Yeah, it feels good to me too. And it might take us a while to really get the routines down, so if you don't mind, I might just spend the night at Ashley's. I could probably even go to work with her in the morning and sort of start figuring out all the stuff at the store."

"That's a good idea. I heard the weather forecast and they're predicting there might be an ice storm later on tonight. I think I'd feel better knowing you weren't driving home late."

"An ice storm?"

"Yeah, it's supposed to rain and then freeze. Pretty bad driving conditions."

Well, this made me hesitate. Did I really want to get stuck driving home in an ice storm? But, on the other hand, if this were my big chance to win Timothy back, maybe I wouldn't even be driving home at all.

"You okay, honey?" My mom was peering at me with a funny look.

"Yeah, just spacing, I guess. I need to go get some things ready to take over to Ashley's."

My mom smiled. "I'm proud of you, Jordan."

"Really?" Now, for whatever reason, that only made me feel worse. I went up to my room and carefully reread Timothy's email. I considered calling Kara and asking her advice, but I knew exactly what she would say. Instead, I picked up the photograph of the cheerleaders and stared blankly at it. Shawna's smirking smile seemed to be taunting me, as if she were daring me to try to take her man. How could I possibly turn away now?

I wasn't totally sure at what point that little green monster had really taken hold of me, but there was no denying that I was pretty much consumed with jealousy and bitterness. And why shouldn't I be? I mean, really, wasn't *I* the victim here?

I had done *everything* I could think of to patch things up with Shawna early on. Man, I'd even given her my Beatles collection! Argh! And then she used me when I had honestly believed she was my friend. And what about the sweater I let her buy before the party where she stole my boyfriend?

But did she care that she totally crushed me and broke my heart? Not even. She only did everything possible to torment me and make my life worse. She stole my car keys and my best pair of jeans. And everyone knows she's the real reason I'm on probation right now. I mean, this girl is evil. The way I see it, she really has it coming to her, and the only way I can ever get even is to win Timothy back.

The way I see it, it's a win-win situation for me. Hurt Shawna and get Timothy. But it's a win-win for Tim too. He gets rid of the twisted devil chick and gets a girlfriend who's really worthy of him—a girlfriend who knows how to listen and really understands him.

And suddenly I knew I had to settle this thing, once and for all. I was in and Shawna was out. Nothing was going to stop me.

And so, with *that* kind of determination, I carefully dressed in my coolest outfit and packed a small bag for whatever might happen as the evening progressed. I emptied about fifty bucks in small bills and change from my piggy bank, and then without looking back or questioning my motives or my final decision, I set out to meet my true love.

sixteen

IT WASN'T ALL THAT COLD OUT WHEN I STARTED DRIVING. AND THE RAIN was just light and misty. I felt certain that Mom must've heard the wrong weather report—maybe it was for *tomorrow* night. *Besides,* I told myself, *I'm a good driver.* And more important, I was on a mission.

It was just a little past eight when I found and parked in front of the Starbucks on Oak Street. I didn't see Timothy's car anywhere in sight, but then I figured he'd probably walked over. My guess was that the guys would be staying at a dorm on campus. I had even wondered if Timothy might possibly have a place where I could crash for the night, especially if the weather got worse. I wasn't totally sure this would be *the* night when we would actually have sex for the first time. But I was certainly open to that possibility since apparently that was the only way to seal the deal with this guy. Mostly I tried not to think about that too much.

I ran across the street through the pouring rain. It felt like sharp needles as it hit my face, and I could tell there was ice mixed in. Maybe my mom had been right after all. But I didn't have time to think about that as I shook my hair off. Then, holding my head high, I walked into the coffee shop, smiling and confident and ready for anything. But as I glanced around, I didn't see Timothy anywhere.

I did notice a guy who looked a lot like Brett Hawkins, at least from the back. He was standing at the counter ordering something. I stepped closer to see that it was indeed Brett. And that's when I figured that Timothy must be on his way. Or perhaps he was in the restroom or hiding somewhere and waiting to pop out at me.

"Hey, Brett," I said with a friendly smile.

"Jordan!" He turned around with a pleased smile. "You made it!"

"Yeah."

"Man, I thought with the cruddy weather and everything—"

"No problem." I waved my hand and glanced back to where the restrooms were located, hoping to see Tim emerging any minute.

"Can I get you something?"

"Sure, thanks. I'll have a double espresso."

He grinned. "Cool."

I nodded. "Might as well get wired, right?"

He nodded. "Why not?"

"I guess I'll go sit and wait," I told him, unsure as to whether I should ask about Timothy yet or not. Suddenly, I wondered if perhaps Timothy had chickened out and sent Brett over to tell me I'd been dumped—again. But then Brett seemed to be in a pretty good mood. He didn't exactly look like he was playing the bearer of bad news.

Finally, he came back over and sat down with our two coffees. "So, how's it going?"

"Okay, considering."

"Yeah, it's been kind of a hard year for you."

"You could say that again."

He grinned. "Well, maybe it's about time it all turned around."

I nodded. "Fine by me."

I was just about to ask him about Timothy, but he spoke first.

"That was a really cool email you sent last night."

Had Tim actually let Brett read my email? How humiliating! Even so, I sort of nodded, unsure of the correct response under these circumstances.

"You haven't changed your mind or anything?" He looked slightly troubled.

"Changed my mind?"

"Yeah. About me and you."

"Me and you?"

He smiled. "Well, that's what you said in your email."

"My email?"

Now he shook his head. "Are you okay, Jordan? You seem a little loopy."

I took a big sip of the espresso to hide my confusion, scalding my tongue as I did but keeping my eyes on Brett the whole time. What on earth was this guy up to? What kind of game was he playing?

"I'm kind of lost," I confessed.

"Yeah, that's sort of how I felt at first. But then after I considered it, I wondered why I'd never thought about it before. I mean, I like Ashley okay, but she's not anything like you, Jordan. Sometimes I actually think she's a little depressed or something. But you always seem so cheerful and up. Think about all the crud Timothy and Shawna have put you through. You just keep bouncing right back with that sweet little smile on your face." He grinned now. "I really like that."

Okay, Abbie and I used to watch these ancient reruns of this totally lame old show called *The Twilight Zone*, and I seriously felt like that was exactly where I had landed tonight. Like, who am I? And how did I get here? Still, I hate looking totally stupid and ignorant, so I continued to just play along.

"Now, I can't remember exactly what I wrote in that email, Brett. You know how you just whip something out and send it?"

"Yeah. I've sent stuff that I wished I hadn't. But mostly you just said how you'd been watching me and thinking how we belonged together. But what really got my attention was when you told me that Ashley is tired of me and about to dump me for Caleb Andrews."

I'm thinking this is total bunk because I know without a doubt that Ashley is head over heels for this guy. But feeling thoroughly confused, I don't say this.

"And which email address did I send it from?"

"Huh?"

"You know, I have a couple that I use."

"I don't remember it exactly, but it did have the word 'blondie' in it."

"Oh, yeah." I nodded, although I had no such email address. Someone, and I could guess who, was playing a really bad joke on me. And Brett too. But how was I supposed to get out of this stupid mess gracefully? I didn't want to hurt this guy's feelings. And I suppose I was just slightly flattered that he was actually interested in me. I mean, who would've thought someone like Brett Hawkins would like *me*? But at the same time, I was totally infuriated that it wasn't Timothy sitting here with me right now. And why had he sent me that email inviting me to meet him tonight? Of *course*, I suddenly realized, he *hadn't* sent it at all. *Shawna had.*

"Brett, I need to tell you something."

He nodded. "Shoot."

"I think I may have made a mistake in coming here tonight."

He frowned.

"Yeah, it was one of those things that seemed right at the time. You know, like sending an email and then regretting it? And I think you're a totally cool guy, and I would be so lucky to have someone like you. But this is the wrong way to get you."

He nodded. "Yeah, I kind of know what you mean."

"And besides that, Ashley really *does* like you."

"How do you know?"

"She talks about you all the time, Brett. You're the only thing about high school that she doesn't seemed bored with."

"Really?"

"Really."

"And you're pretty good friends with her?"

"Sort of."

Now he really frowned. "Well, if you're such good friends with her, why did you come here tonight?"

I sighed. Good question. Why had I come here tonight? If I told him the truth, he'd feel stupid and used. If I lied, I'd look like the backstabbing tramp that Shawna accused me of being. As it turned out, I didn't get the chance to do either.

"See!" cried Shawna as she and Ashley walked into the Starbucks and quickly came straight to our table.

The look on Ashley's face was like nothing I'd ever seen before—a mixture of deep hurt and pure white rage. I mean, if I thought I'd had jealousy problems with Shawna, I knew I'd hit the mother lode with Ashley. I stood up and tried to explain. "It's not what you think—"

"Save it for someone who gives a—"

"It's really not," said Brett, trying to grab Ashley's hand. "She was just telling me—"

Then *smack!* Ashley slapped Brett right across the face. I

couldn't believe it. And fearing I would be next, I took a step backward and headed toward the door. I considered saying something to Ashley to straighten things out. I wanted to shout, "This is all just a setup!" but I had a feeling my words would be lost on this crowd. Now Brett was yelling at Ashley and Shawna was throwing the blame at me. All I could think was, *I better get out of here, and fast.* Hopefully, Brett and I would have a chance to sort things out later after tempers had cooled.

I knew that the temperature had dropped drastically when I went outside and immediately slipped on the ice that was quickly building up on the street. I glanced back to the scene in Starbucks and could tell they were still fighting. I think I expected them to come after me at any moment. I hurried to unlock my ice-encrusted car and then, without bothering to scrape off my windshield, turned the key in the ignition. It was clear that the wipers were useless and I could barely see, but somehow I drove down the street and managed to find the highway out of town.

By then my little defroster had managed to burn two small holes through the ice on my windshield. Hunching forward like an old woman, I slowly made my way onto the highway. But my hands were still shaking uncontrollably. I tried not to think about what had just happened. Instead, I told myself to focus on the highway ahead of me. I knew the roads were slick and suspected that I should move slowly in my frosted blue Bug. To my relief, the other cars were keeping their speed down too. And because I had absolutely no experience driving on ice—and not a whole lot of experience driving, period—I figured I'd better follow their example.

My head was being scorched by my defroster, which I had to keep running on high in order to keep the ice off my windshield, and my stomach was tied in so many knots that I honestly felt like

I might need to pull over and throw up.

How have you gotten yourself into this stupid mess? I asked myself as I crawled along the highway like a frozen turtle. *How could you be such a total fool?*

Of course, I had no answers for myself—only more and more questions. And it wasn't long before my questions turned into hateful accusations.

"You are such a totally worthless loser," I told myself aloud. "You are the worst friend on the planet. First you totally ditch your best friend just so you can hang with a bunch of kids who probably hate your guts. But still, you don't give up, do you? You're playing this game, thinking you can win, and all you do is make more messes out of everything. And then you go and make those messes bigger and bigger."

I figured I was pretty much like the Cat in the Hat. No matter what he did to clean it up, the pink-spot mess he had made only got worse and worse—well, until he pulled out Little Cat Z. But I didn't happen to have a Little Cat Z under my hat. All I had was stupid old mess-making me.

"This is just what you deserve," I yelled at myself. "After all, you only think about yourself! You are pathetic and shallow and selfish and totally stupid. And do you know why you're stuck with your own company tonight, Jordan? It's because no one else can stand to be around you."

But even though it was a form of venting, and most likely quite true, these harsh accusations didn't make me feel one bit better. I considered calling Kara just then and pouring out my guts to her, although I felt pretty certain that talking on my cell phone while driving on a road that was slicker than a giant ice rink would be pushing things a bit. Plus, I didn't see any place to pull over at the moment.

But if I could've called Kara just then, I think I would've asked her about this whole God thing. I would've said, "Okay, Kara, *where* is God when I need him? Because I'm telling you, I could use some serious help right now. I've made a total mess of everything, and like those kids who needed Little Cat Z, I could really use some real live assistance right now. So tell me, Kara, is God like Little Cat Z? Can he clean this mess up? And if he can, *where* can you find him when you need him?"

"Help me, God!" I finally screamed at the top of my lungs. "Do something about my pathetically messed-up life!" Then, in pure frustration, I socked the steering wheel. Big mistake.

When I came to, I was still inside my car, but my car didn't look anything like it used to look. It's like the outside had come into the inside, and I was pinned somewhere in between. I was shivering with cold and feeling extreme pain everywhere, but mostly in my right foot. I could tell by headlights moving off to my left that I had gone off the highway and hit something, maybe a tree, although it was hard to tell since my own headlights were knocked out. But I was far enough from the road that I didn't know if anyone would ever notice me, and I couldn't see my purse, which of course held my cell phone.

"Oh, God," I cried out. "I mean it this time. Please, please, help me. I'm sorry I've made such a mess." Then I think I must've passed out again.

The next time I came to, I was in another kind of vehicle, or maybe it was a bubble, because it was filled with this bluish sort of light. And it was warm and I was wrapped in something and there was this young woman looking down at me. "How you doing, sweetie?" she asked in a voice so kind that I thought maybe she was actually an angel.

"I've been better," I said, but it sounded like someone else, or maybe a frog. Then I closed my eyes and prepared to meet my maker or, more likely, someone else who ruled in another sort of place. Despite the comforting warmth of the blanket, that thought chilled me to the soul.

seventeen

MY PARENTS WAITED UNTIL I WAS FEELING A LITTLE BETTER BEFORE THEY popped the big question.

"Jordan, we need to know something," my dad said in a tightly controlled voice. "What on earth were you doing sixty miles from home last night?" I had to admire his restraint since I suspect that he really wanted to yell.

"Especially after I told you there was going to be an ice storm," pleaded my mom. "You said you were going to Ashley's. What were you doing?"

"And what were you thinking?" demanded my dad.

I closed my eyes and leaned back onto the hospital bed. They'd finally moved me from the emergency room when they discovered there was nothing life-threateningly wrong with me and that I'd miraculously suffered only a broken ankle and a blow to the head— well, that and lots of cuts and bruises. Some miracle if you ask me.

"Are you okay, honey?" My mom's voice was softer now, like the empathy factor had just kicked in again.

I opened my eyes and looked at them. I could tell they were still freaked about this whole thing. And I'm sure it must be awful to get a phone call like that from the state police. "Like I said, I am really, really sorry about this. I feel bad to have worried you guys."

"We're just relieved you're okay," said Mom.

"And extremely curious as to what you were up to."

"I know. And I'll tell you, but it's a long story." I sighed. "And I'm not sure I can even get it straight right now." I closed my eyes again. "I'm just so tired."

"You might as well get some rest," said my mom. "They want to keep you here for observation until morning anyway."

"You guys go home," I told them with eyes still shut, probably trying to play the brave victim for their benefit. "I'll be fine."

"No." I could tell that my mom felt it would be wrong to leave me here.

I opened my eyes. "Really, *go home*. There's nothing you can do for me. I'm going to be perfectly fine."

"Well, I suppose we could still get a few hours of sleep," said Dad as he glanced at the clock on the wall.

"Yes," I assured them. "Please do. It'll make me feel better. And believe me, I already feel bad enough as it is."

"And you'll tell us the whole story tomorrow?" asked my dad.

"I promise." And I actually meant it. I'd reached the place where I was totally sick of all my lies and my manipulations and my whole messed-up life. Why should I even care if everyone knew everything about me? Maybe I'd take out an ad in the paper and tell the world what a stupid, freaking idiot I really am. But at the moment, I only wanted to sleep and escape all the crud that was heaped up around me.

Morning came too soon, and with it my parents—only now they were showered and combed and dressed like normal people, something of a relief actually. As we drove home on roads that had already thawed, I told them the whole gruesome story. And to my surprise, it was a relief to get it out in the open. I wondered why I hadn't done this much sooner.

"Wow!" said my dad, shaking his head in parental amazement.

"With friends like that, who needs enemies?" said my mom with a sigh.

I sighed too. "I realize it was part my fault."

"Well, that's good," said Dad.

"I never thought Shawna was that kind of a girl," said Mom. "She seemed so sweet."

"Parents are always the last ones to know what's really going on or what kids are really like," I told them.

"That's reassuring," said Dad.

"It's the truth."

"Speaking of the truth," said Mom. "I always considered you to be a pretty honest person, Jordan. Of all four kids, I always felt I could count on you to be truthful to me. When did that all change?"

"I guess it was just part of my desperate attempt to get Timothy back, like I was willing to do whatever it took."

"Do you still feel like that?" asked Mom in a hesitant voice, like maybe she really didn't want to hear my answer.

"To be perfectly honest, I don't know how I feel. Or maybe I'm feeling so many things that I can't figure out which feeling is worth paying attention to."

"That's understandable," said Dad. "You've been through a lot."

"How's the pain?" asked Mom. "It's almost time for another pill."

"I'll be okay until we get home."

"We didn't want to tell you last night," began Dad, "but the police told us that your car was totaled."

"Just like my life." And then I started to cry.

"Oh, honey," said my mom, turning around in the front seat to look at me. "It's not as bad as it seems. Last night I was praying for you—"

"You were praying?"

"Yes, I happen to pray sometimes. Why?"

"Well, I know we go to church sometimes, but I guess I never really thought you guys took it very seriously."

"You don't know everything about us," said Dad, giving me the impression that maybe he prays too.

"Anyway, as I was praying it occurred to me that God may have had a hand in this, Jordan. Maybe he's trying to get your attention."

"Why didn't he just kill me?" I said with sarcasm. "That might've been easier."

"Oh, honey," said Mom. "You don't really mean that."

"My life is over anyway," I continued. "I might as well be dead."

"The policeman at the hospital said it's a miracle you're not dead," said Dad. "In fact, he made me feel a little guilty for allowing you to get that VW Bug at all."

"I *loved* that car!"

"Yeah, but the policeman said it crumpled like tinfoil when you hit that stump. He didn't understand how you didn't crumple with it."

"It was just a stump?" I asked incredulously. "It felt like a massive tree or a brick wall."

"Good thing it wasn't," said Mom. "You probably *would* be dead."

"They had to use the Jaws of Life to get you out."

"Really?" I considered this. "Too bad I missed it."

"How's your head, honey?"

"Kind of achy."

What I really wanted to say was "kind of messed up." I mean, I know I wasn't thinking too straight before last night, but now it's like I can hardly think straight at all. It's like my head is filled up with this cloud of confusion and it's going to take me forever to be able to sort it all out and see clearly again. I'm hoping this might be partially the result of my concussion and the meds, but I'm afraid it's mostly due to me and my stupid choices of late.

And yet I'm not sure what the answer is to my confusion. Right now all I have are more questions. Questions, questions, questions.

Like who is really my friend? Certainly not Shawna, and not even Ashley now, and probably none of the girls on the cheerleading squad after they hear what I "did." And certainly not Timothy. He might've even been in cahoots with Shawna's little sting operation. Not Brett either. Poor guy, he is in almost as much hot water as I am. Maybe I should have handled things differently last night, before the girls got there. But what good would that have done in the end? Kara may still be my friend, but even so, I get the feeling that we're just too different to be close anymore. Of course, there are always my parents. But that's different.

And then I think about cheerleading. I had invested so much time and energy in getting on the squad, and now it looks as if I'm going to be laid up for most of basketball season. I might as well quit.

And then there are my grades. I don't even want to think about them right now. Although here is one consolation: Being laid up with this stupid foot, I might actually have time to do some homework and salvage my GPA. Still, what good is a GPA if you have no life, no friends, nothing?

Then there's the God question. And here's what's really troubling me: When I cried out to God for help, I ended up in an accident that could've killed me. Now, if that's God's way of helping, well, like my mom said, "With friends like that, who needs enemies?"

So there you have it, the messed-up life of Jordan Ferguson. What a stinking pile of crud.

eighteen

"YOU HAVE VISITORS," SAID MOM.

"Huh?" I'd spent most of Monday just resting in bed, putting off the inevitable (returning to school) for as long as possible. I'd even mentioned the idea of homeschool, but my mom was not enthusiastic.

"Visitors."

"*Mom.*" I gave her a warning look as in, "Do not let anyone in this room," and then attempted to smooth my hair just in case she wasn't listening. "Don't you get it? I don't want to see *anyone* right now."

"It's just me," called a voice I instantly recognized as Kara's.

"Oh." I shrugged, realizing that it wasn't anyone from the "cool" crowd. "That's okay, I guess I don't mind seeing Kara."

"And Edgar too?" asked Kara as she came through the door.

"*Edgar?*" I gave her my darkest look.

"He gave me a ride. He just wanted to say hey."

I rolled my eyes and leaned back on my pillows. "Sure, whatever."

"Man, you look awful," said Kara as she sat at the end of my bed.

"Thanks."

"Sorry."

"Everyone at school was talking about you today," said Edgar.

I peered curiously at him. Now I just can't seem to figure this guy out.

"How would *you* know?" I snapped at him, feeling rather mean.

Kara laughed. "Edgar knows everything. I almost always get my information from him, and nine times out of ten, he's right on the money."

He shrugged. "Thanks."

"Nine times out of ten?"

"Oh, I don't know," said Edgar with a shy smile.

"So tell me, Edgar," I said in a sickeningly sweet voice, "how is it that you know *everything?*"

"I guess I'm just a good listener."

"He says it's because people don't usually notice that he's around or don't think he's paying any attention, but he is," explained Kara.

I guess that sort of made sense. I do remember thinking it was odd the way Shawna or Ashley would continue talking about some of the most private things while some nerdy sort of girl was just standing there listening, like the girl was deaf or something. I just didn't get that.

"So, what are they saying about me?" I asked. "Not that I really want to know."

"Well, there are a lot of different stories floating around," began Edgar.

"That's why I wanted to come over here and see you for myself," said Kara. "Edgar even overheard someone say that you tried to kill yourself."

I attempted what came out as a pretty pitiful laugh. "It figures."

"Some kids were saying that you were nearly killed in an

accident. And others were saying you're paralyzed from the neck down," said Kara.

"Some even said you were trying to commit suicide after being caught trying to steal your best friend's boyfriend," added Edgar.

"Great." I groaned as I tried to pull myself up higher in my bed.

"Here, let me help," said Kara. And she and Edgar both helped me get more comfortable.

"Thanks. Did they say anything else?"

"Some thought you were in a coma," said Edgar.

"What were my, uh, friends saying?" I knew using the word *friends* was stretching it a bit.

"Well, I didn't hear everything," admitted Edgar, "but it seemed there was a division of sorts."

"A division?"

"Yeah. Some of your friends were acting like you deserved what you got, primarily Shawna and Ashley. Maybe Betsy Mosler too."

"But she's such a follower," said Kara.

"But there were others, like Amber and Jenny and some of the guys, who felt really bad for you."

"But does anyone know what really happened that night?" I asked them.

"What do you mean?" asked Kara.

I considered this. Did I really want to tell Kara, and Edgar of all people, how I got totally stung by Shawna Frye? Admitting as much to my parents was one thing, but telling these guys would be pretty humiliating.

"Can I trust you guys?"

"Of course," said Kara. And I knew she meant it.

Edgar nodded. And it was weird, but somehow I understood, perhaps by the serious look in his eyes, that I could trust him too.

"It's a long story," I began.

"We have time," said Edgar as he pulled up a chair.

And so I told them the whole embarrassing story. And by the time I reached the end, I was crying again.

Kara actually took my hand. "I'm so sorry, Jordan. That really sucks."

"I, I know." I said. "And I thought these guys were my friends."

Kara shook her head. "I tried to warn you, Jordan. I told you they were evil."

"They're not evil," said Edgar in a quiet voice.

We both turned and stared at him.

"What do you mean?" I demanded, ready to throw this nerd out of my bedroom for treason.

"They're just doing it all wrong," he said. "And no offense, but so are you."

"What do you mean?" I demanded again. Hopefully, I wasn't expected to be clever or original when I was in this kind of condition.

"I mean that you guys are living life for yourselves. You're leaving God totally out of it, and as a result things can get pretty messed up."

Well, I couldn't deny that things were pretty messed up, but I wasn't about to admit to anything either.

"That's true," said Kara. "I only figured it out recently, but since I invited God into my life, things have been changing."

"I'll say." I rolled my eyes.

"And you've been changing too," she reminded me.

"Yeah, you mentioned that already."

"And do you like the changes?" asked Edgar.

"What are you guys?" I asked. "A pair of religious shrinks? Maybe you should get yourselves a TV show on that weird church network where everyone has big hair and too much mascara."

Edgar laughed. "Hey, that might be kinda cool."

"We're just trying to help," said Kara in a defensive tone. "We can leave if you want."

I waved my hand. "No, I don't want you to leave. I'm sorry, I guess I'm just feeling pretty bummed and cranky right now."

"Understandable," said Edgar.

I nodded, liking this guy more.

"Is there anything we can do for you?" he asked.

"Huh?"

"Any way we can help you?"

I shrugged and then said, "Yeah, go tell all my so-called friends that I was framed."

He smiled. "That could probably be arranged."

"Yeah, I'm sure." My sarcasm was back now.

"You never know, Jordan," said Kara. "Edgar has these ways of making things happen."

"By praying to God?" I eyed him now.

"Sometimes." He smiled. "And sometimes by letting the truth come to light."

"Well, I wish someone would let the truth come to light about how Shawna set me up on Saturday night. I mean, sheesh, it's not like I wasn't making a fine mess of my life without any help. But why did Shawna feel such a need to help me out?"

"Because she was threatened," offered Edgar.

"Yeah, sure." I acted like I was bored, even though I was really listening.

"You're a cool girl, Jordan," said Edgar. "Shawna believed you had what it took to steal her guy, and she wanted to make sure that you didn't."

"She probably wanted you totally out of commission," added Kara.

"She figured if she destroyed your reputation, got you in trouble with cheerleading, and ruined your strongest friendship with Ashley Crow, she might actually have the upper hand."

"And the nearly fatal car wreck was just the icing on the cake," I added.

"Exactly."

"Almost as if God was on her side?" I suggested.

"Oh, I don't think so," said Edgar.

"Why not?" I demanded. "Look at her. She's still got Timothy, she's still cheerleading, and she has friends. She's on top, and I'm not. If anything, I'm buried beneath a great big pile of—"

"Only temporarily," said Edgar.

"Huh?"

"You're down now, Jordan, but only for a while. I think God is giving you a chance to really look at your life and decide just how you want to live it."

"That's right," said Kara. "You can keep on living it for yourself or invite God to take over."

"Take over?"

"It's not like he takes control of you," said Edgar. "You still have to make the choices. He'll just help you make better ones."

"He has a plan for your life," Kara added.

I shook my head. "Here we go again. The Peebles and Hendricks Evangelism Hour."

Kara winked at Edgar. "I kind of like the sound of that, don't you?"

He grinned. "Maybe we should take it on the road."

"Yeah, we could set up a tent and—"

"Come on, you guys," I said.

"Sorry." Kara returned her attention to me. "I just don't see why, especially after all this, you're not even interested in giving God a try."

I sat there in silence for a long moment, considering whether or not to tell them, but finally I couldn't help myself.

"I *did* give God a try!" I shouted. "And he let me down."

"What do you mean?" asked Edgar.

"Look, I was really feeling bad that night—after Shawna set me up—and I was driving home on that ice and actually cried out to God. I *begged* him to help me!"

"And?"

"And I got in that stupid wreck, totaled my car, and am stuck here in bed with this broken ankle."

"So you think that's God's fault?" asked Edgar.

"I'm not sure *what* I think."

"Do you think God wanted you to go meet Timothy that night?" asked Kara.

I considered this. "Probably not."

"What actually caused the wreck, Jordan?" asked Edgar.

"What do you mean?"

"Was it another car? Or what?"

Suddenly I remembered the one little detail I hadn't told anyone yet—not even my parents. "I guess it was me."

"But it was icy," said Kara as if to defend me.

"Yeah. It *was* icy. But I was so furious about the Shawna setup that when I was crying out to God, asking him to be my Little Cat Z, well, I just slammed my fist into the steering wheel." I looked up at them with what I'm sure must've been a pretty sheepish expression.

Edgar just nodded. "I can understand how you would've been that frustrated after everything that happened to you, Jordan."

"Really?" I felt just slightly hopeful.

"So, in a way, you probably had more to do with causing that accident than God," suggested Kara.

"I guess."

"Can I ask you a question?" Kara looked slightly confused.

"Sure."

"What is Little Cat Z?"

"Didn't you ever read Dr. Seuss?" I asked her.

"*The Cat in the Hat!*" said Edgar suddenly. "It was even a movie, Kara. Didn't you see it?"

"You mean that kids' movie?" asked Kara.

"Yeah, but it was pretty cool."

I nodded, feeling kind of silly for relating God to something created for children. "Little Cat Z is the one who finally comes in and cleans up the big mess," I explained.

"And you think God is going to be like Little Cat Z?" asked Edgar.

"Maybe."

"Hmmm." He seemed to be considering this.

"I definitely think God can help you clean up this mess," said Kara. "But you've got to do your part too. Anyway, that's how it was with me."

"And with me too," added Edgar.

"I guess I kind of figured as much."

"So, you've really been giving God some thought?" asked Kara hopefully.

I shrugged. "It's kind of hard not to when you're not sure whether you're going to live or die. There were several moments, like when I was trapped in my car, and then in the ambulance, when I got really, really scared about what would happen to me if I did die. So, to be perfectly honest, I have been giving God some serious thought. But I was kind of mad at him too."

"Because you thought he'd let you down?" asked Edgar.

"I guess so. I remembered crying out for help, but I suppose I sort of forgot about hitting the steering wheel."

"That's usually how it goes," said Edgar. "It's easier to blame God than to face up to who we really are."

"Who we really are?" I echoed.

"Sometimes it's confusing, huh?" said Kara.

"You're telling me." I leaned my head back on my pillows now. "Hey, you guys have been really cool and everything. And I'm sorry I'm such a grump. But I am getting kind of tired and my head is aching again—"

"Hey, no problem," said Edgar, standing quickly and pulling Kara to her feet. "We didn't mean to wear you out with our Peebles and Hendricks road show."

I smiled. "Thanks, you guys. You've given me a lot to think about."

Then Kara did something she'd never done before, and she and I had been best friends since kindergarten. She leaned over and kissed me on the cheek. "I love you, Jordan," she said, "and I'll be praying for you."

I nodded, but the lump growing in my throat made it impossible to answer.

"Take it easy," called Edgar.

After they left, I felt hot tears streaming down both my cheeks. But these were not my usual tears of anger or frustration or even that deep green jealousy. These felt like tears of relief, like maybe there was hope for me after all.

nineteen

I MANAGED TO TALK MOM INTO LETTING ME STAY HOME FROM SCHOOL FOR a couple more days. "My head still aches," I told her, which was true. "Besides, I can catch up on my homework and maybe get my grades back up there."

And I am trying to be true to my word about the homework, but I must admit that the soaps are somewhat distracting. I've developed this weird fascination for watching characters who seem more messed up than I am. Of course, I have to remind myself, they are just actors. This is my life.

On Tuesday evening, Amber dropped by. She brought a bouquet of yellow roses, supposedly from the whole cheerleading squad, although I have my suspicions that not everyone contributed.

"Now I heard something weird today, Jordan," she told me as she sat down on my bed. Then looking around my room she said, "Man, your room is sure neat. Do you guys have a maid or something?"

I smiled. "I'm sort of obsessive about it. A neat freak, you know."

"I wish I were a little more like that. Anyway, I heard this *thing* today, and I wanted to ask you, face-to-face, whether it was true or not."

"What's that?"

"Well, there's a new rumor going around that Shawna actually set you up to get caught with Brett the night you got into that wreck. And some people are even saying that Shawna is the one who actually caused your wreck. Is any of this true?"

"Some of it."

Amber leaned forward, her large brown eyes even bigger than usual. "What happened?"

"First of all, the wreck *wasn't* Shawna's fault. Someone at the rumor mill must've gotten carried away." But then I thought about this for a moment. "Although, in a way I suppose she is partially responsible. I mean, if she hadn't set me up, I wouldn't have been out driving in that crazy ice storm. But then again, it was my choice to go."

"Okay, but what about the rest of it? Did she really set you up?"

So I told Amber the whole setup story, and she was totally stunned. "No way!" she said in amazement.

"Way." I nodded. "You can even check my email if you don't believe me. I saved what was sent, supposedly from Timothy. Maybe he was even in cahoots with Shawna, but now I'm not so sure. She might've gotten his password without him knowing. But it definitely came from his email address. And until I realized it was all a stupid trick, I believed it was legit."

"Have you asked Timothy about this?"

I shook my head. "What difference does it make now?"

"I don't know. But if it were me, I'd want to know."

"It's all so humiliating."

"Yeah, I'll bet. But if the real truth comes out and the stuff hits the fan, it's Shawna who's going to look cruddy, not you."

"Do you think?"

"I know."

"I wish that were true. But in the meantime, it's hard to want to show my face at school."

"When are you coming back?"

"Maybe on Thursday, or even Friday if I'm lucky—although my mom's starting to push me."

"Do you mind if I take a look at that email?" she asked. "Not that I don't believe you, but I think we need to get this thing nailed."

So I climbed out of bed and hobbled over to my computer, opened it up, and showed her the email.

"Wow, that is so weird. I knew Shawna wanted to hold on to Timothy, but I never knew how much trouble she'd go to." Amber turned and looked at me. "By the way, are you sure she took your jeans that day?"

"I really think so. And maybe my car keys too. But I can't prove anything. She just had this look in her eyes."

"And that's the day when you lost it in front of Ms. Brookes in the parking lot?"

"Yeah. Thus my probation." I looked down at the cast on my foot. "Like it matters now. I might as well quit the squad, Amber. Do you think it's too late for the alternate to step in?"

She shrugged. "I don't know. That's not a decision we need to rush."

"I feel really bad that I've messed things up for the cheerleaders," I said. "Well, other than Shawna, that is. But I hope you guys do okay at Flair Fair without me."

"It was tricky reworking the routines for just six girls at first, but it's starting to work. I think we'll be fine. Mostly, we're going to miss your beautiful gymnastics and your lightweight little body at the top of the pyramid."

I tried to smile as I poked myself in the belly. "I don't know about that. I think I've been stress-eating lately. I'll probably weigh a hundred and fifty by the time I get out of this cast."

She laughed. "The chubby cheerleader. Maybe we can just roll you to the top of the pyramid!"

I tried to laugh, but the mental image this conjured was enough to make me choke.

Amber picked up her bag. "Well, maybe it's good if you're not coming back to school tomorrow."

"Why?"

"Gives me time to sort a few things out."

My eyes grew wide now. "With Shawna?"

She nodded. "It's about time someone stood up to that chick."

I nodded. "Well, you're probably the only one who can do it."

She frowned. "Yeah, me and Ms. Brookes."

"You're going to bring Ms. Brookes into it?"

She sighed. "I know it could really mess it up for us, especially at Flair Fair, since Shawna will probably be suspended too, but it's the right thing to do."

It occurred to me then that I probably didn't know Amber as well as I thought I did. "I never knew you were like that, Amber."

"Like what?"

"That you would actually risk something for the cheerleading squad in order to do the right thing."

"Do I come across like I wouldn't?"

Now I felt sort of bad about how that came out. "Not exactly."

"Well, the truth is, I try to live my life in a way that honors God."

I blinked. "You're kidding?"

"What?" she demanded. "I know I have a big mouth and say some incredibly stupid things sometimes. But do I really come across as a complete heathen?"

"Not at all, Amber. I just thought you were too cool to be a Christian."

She laughed. "Now, that's a good one, Jordan. *Too cool to be a Christian.* Can't wait to share that one with Pastor Don."

"That's not exactly what I meant," I tried again. "Maybe it's that you never preach at anyone."

"Hmmm." She rubbed her chin. "I guess it just never occurred to me to do that. Do you like being preached at?"

"Not exactly."

"Well, maybe I'm just a different kind of Christian. Did you ever think of that? Maybe I just want to try to live my life in a way that finally makes someone, maybe someone like you, stop and take notice and say to me, 'Hey, Amber, girl, what you got going that I don't got?' You ever considered that?"

I nodded. "Well, I noticed that you manage to avoid the petty stuff, the viciousness. You seem to have higher standards than the rest of us. I guess I just assumed that was because you were trying to set a good example since you're captain and all."

"Well, that's true enough. You guys have been something else this year. I'm sure glad I'm a senior. I'm getting way too old for this kind of nonsense."

"I'm sorry, Amber."

She smiled. "It's okay. Besides, I think Shawna has more to do with this than you do. You just got caught in a bad spot."

"And I made some bad choices too."

She nodded. "Yeah, that's true. But maybe you learned, eh?"

"I hope so."

"Well, take care. And hopefully I'll see you on Thursday or Friday."

"Thanks, Amber."

twenty

I WASN'T ALL THAT SURPRISED WHEN KARA AND EDGAR CAME TO SEE ME on Wednesday.

"I thought you'd be back in school today," said Kara.

"If I had my way, I'd never go back at all," I snapped at her. I was feeling pretty grumpy. My mom had taken Leah to her piano lesson. I hadn't even had a shower, my hair was nasty, and I basically felt like something green and fuzzy that you might find in the back of your refrigerator after being gone on vacation for a couple of weeks.

"Sorry," she said. "Do you want us to leave?"

"No. I'm just feeling sorry for myself."

"That is so unlike you, Jordan. Or at least who you *used* to be. You were the one who was always pulling me up by my bootstraps. You were Little Merry Sunshine who always sang things like, 'The sun'll come out tomorrow.'"

I groaned in real agony.

"She would actually do that, *for real,*" Kara told Edgar.

"Yeah, yeah, kick me when I'm down. Why not just get a club and break my other foot?"

"Why are you so bummed?" asked Kara more gently.

"*Look at me!*" I held out my arms as if to make my point. I was wearing a nasty old T-shirt, some baggy pajama bottoms, no makeup, and hair that looked like fettuccini Alfredo. "Why shouldn't I be bummed?"

"I've seen you looking better," agreed Kara. "But who cares when you're just slumming around the house anyway?"

"Yeah, that's a great comfort coming from you. Your idea of fashion is to put on a clean pair of socks."

Kara frowned.

"I'm sorry," I said. "It just feels like years since I had a shower, and my foot itches, and the mere suggestion of going to school tomorrow just totally freaks me."

"Want me to help you with a shower?" she offered.

I was tempted, but then glanced over at Edgar. "Does *he* have to help too?"

He laughed. "I'm not even going to respond to *that*. I'll be downstairs if you ladies need me."

"Thanks."

So, Kara actually helped me to wrap my foot up in plastic and take a nice long shower. She patiently helped me shampoo and condition my hair and then even shaved my legs!

"I think you got almost as wet as I did," I said as I sat on the stool and toweled off.

"Next time I'll bring my swimsuit."

"Or just go in the buff," I teased, although I know Kara's one of those prim girls who doesn't like undressing in front of anyone.

Before long, I was dressed and we were back in my bedroom. "You want to invite Edgar back up?" I asked as I combed out my hair.

"Do you really want him to come back up?" she asked. "I mean, he mostly just comes along to give me a ride. You don't have to—"

"I happen to like him, Kara," I said in a voice that sounded like, "Duh!"

"Well *okay.*" She smiled and then went out in the hallway and yelled for Edgar to come up.

"Feeling better?" asked Edgar.

"Yeah. Kara's great in the shower."

She rolled her eyes.

"So, how's it going otherwise?" asked Edgar as he pulled up a chair.

I just shrugged.

"Have you given any more thought to the whole God thing?" asked Kara.

"Did you know that Amber Elliot is a Christian?" I asked them. I was still slightly stunned by this news.

"No," said Kara. "I always thought she was kind of mouthy and rude."

"She's definitely outspoken and sort of bossy," I said. "But out of all the cheerleaders, she always seemed to have the highest standards, although I know she's not perfect."

"That's cool," said Edgar. "Just because a person is a Christian doesn't mean they're perfect. I can attest to that."

"Me too," said Kara. "You should've heard what I said to Bree last night when I found out she'd borrowed my favorite Gap sweater."

"That cool one that I picked out for you last summer?"

"Yeah. She came into my room while I was gone and just took it."

"Man, I would've let her have it."

"That's just what I did." Then Kara frowned. "But I felt lousy afterward. I had to apologize. In fact, I told her if she liked the sweater that much, she could keep it."

"No way!" I shook my head in total disbelief. "You gave her that sweater? That was one of your coolest pieces of clothing, Kara." I wanted to say, "And you don't have many," but I managed to control myself.

"Yeah, I know. But it's just a sweater, Jordan. Bree is my sister."

"Wow." I knew I wouldn't be so nice if Leah did that to me.

"My point is," said Kara, "I still blow it. Over and over and over, I blow it."

"And Jesus forgives us," added Edgar, "over and over and over."

"You guys really should take this act on the road," I said.

"It's *not* an act," said Kara indignantly.

"Yeah, I know. I was trying to be funny. Sorry."

"I was thinking about what you said Monday," said Edgar suddenly, "and it occurred to me that Jesus really *is* kind of like Little Cat Z."

"Huh?"

"It's like he was inside of God's hat, and his purpose was to clean up messes."

"I don't get it."

"Well, we manage to turn life into a complete mess without him, right?"

"I guess."

"And in a way, it's a good thing. I mean, if you were all squeaky clean and perfect, you wouldn't need Little Cat Z, right?"

"I guess not."

"But the fact that you're a mess means you do."

"So you like my Little Cat Z analogy?"

Edgar scratched his head. "Well, I'm not really a theologian, Jordan. But I suppose I believe that God is more like the big cat—not that he makes the messes exactly, because he doesn't. But maybe he allows them to happen just so we'll know that we need Little Cat Z."

And suddenly, right there in my bedroom between Edgar Peebles and Dr. Seuss, it all began to fall into place. It actually started to make sense.

"I think I get it," I said.

"You're kidding!" Kara looked astonished. "I don't even get it. But then I never did read Dr. Seuss."

"No, it really makes sense to me," I said. "I think I want this thing, you guys. I think I really want for Jesus to clean me up. What do I do?"

So they told me how to ask Jesus into my heart, and right there in my bedroom with Kara and Edgar by my side, I followed Edgar's prayer and invited Jesus to come into my life.

"Amen," said Edgar.

"Amen," I repeated and then opened my eyes.

"Wow," said Kara.

"Should I feel different?" I asked.

"Not necessarily," said Edgar. "Some people do, some don't."

"I did," said Kara. "It was really amazing."

"I didn't," said Edgar. "Not at first anyway. But after a while I did."

"What do I do now?" I asked.

"Lots of things," said Kara. "Mostly I just started talking to Jesus all the time."

"That's good," said Edgar. "And you'll want to read the Bible to get to know God better."

"You mean Dr. Seuss won't cut it?" I teased.

He smiled. "And you'll want to get involved in some kind of fellowship."

"Fellowship?"

"A church."

I was suddenly excited. "We have a church," I said. "We go sometimes, but not regularly. I guess I could start going regularly."

Edgar nodded. "God will help to show you what to do, Jordan. Mostly, you should do like Kara says and just talk to him."

I smiled. "Okay. I think I like this already." And to my surprise I really *was* feeling better. Oh, I suppose it could've been the shower or just having friends who cared, but I think it was something more too. "I feel pretty good," I told them.

"Cool," said Edgar. "But even if you wake up feeling rotten tomorrow, you need to trust God and talk to him about it."

"That's right," agreed Kara. "That's what I do."

We talked some more, but it was getting close to dinnertime and I knew they needed to get going.

"Thanks so much, you guys!" I told them. "Really! This is so unbelievable!"

Then we all hugged and I could see that Kara had tears in her eyes.

"I'm so happy for you!" she said. "This is so awesome!"

And it is. Totally awesome. I am as amazed as anyone. And I don't feel quite so freaked about going to school tomorrow. Okay, I'm not like all excited, but at least I'm willing.

twenty-one

G OING TO SCHOOL ON T HURSDAY WAS ONE OF THE HARDEST THINGS I'VE ever done. My mom drove me and even helped me get situated with my bag and crutches, but I felt like a total klutz as I made my way toward the main entrance.

And yet it really did help to imagine that God was going with me. I'd taken Kara's advice and started talking to him about *everything*. And it made me feel better, almost as if my life really was falling back into place again. Still, I was worried about facing my so-called friends.

"Jordan," said Amber as soon as she saw me hobbling through the front door on my crutches. "Want some help with your bag?"

"Thanks." I smiled at her. I wanted to tell her what I'd done yesterday, about inviting God into my life, but I decided to wait for the right moment. After all, it had taken her months to tell me.

"Jordan," said Jenny, "how's it going?"

"Okay," I said.

"The word's out," said Amber in a hushed tone.

"Huh?"

"About what Shawna did to you," said Jenny. "What a total witch!"

I nodded, feeling slightly uncomfortable, though I wasn't sure why.

"Everyone's talking about it," said Jenny, glancing over her shoulder. "Some of us think she should get kicked off the squad."

"Jordan!" called a familiar voice.

I shifted my weight on my crutches in order to look the other direction. There was Ashley coming my way. I didn't know whether to say "hey" or try to run for my life, which wouldn't be easy in my case.

"It's okay," she said when she got closer. "Amber set me straight on what *really* happened last weekend."

"I'm so sorry," I told her. "I got caught so totally unaware and I was about to set Brett straight and then you guys showed up. And—"

"I know." Ashley nodded. "Brett tried to explain it to me that night, but I was so furious with him that I wouldn't even listen. Then after Amber explained everything to me yesterday, I went to Brett and he totally confirmed it." She put her arms around me and gave me a gentle squeeze. "I'm sorry, Jordan. I should've known you wouldn't have pulled that kind of stunt."

I just nodded, though I was honestly thinking, *How do you know I wouldn't?* But I wasn't about to rock the boat.

"That's right," agreed Jenny. "We need to remember that Shawna's the Crud Queen."

"I don't think that girl's going to show her face here today," said Ashley.

"I don't blame her," said Amber. "Even Timothy is mad at her."

"Timothy?" I felt myself growing weak.

"Yeah," said Jenny. "Caleb told me that they broke up last night and Timothy said 'never again.'"

"Wow," I said. "I'll bet she's upset."

"Well, she deserves it," said Jenny.

I just nodded. Part of me agreed with Jenny, but a newer part of me wasn't so sure anymore. Part of me was thinking that I wasn't much different than Shawna, but I didn't admit this to anyone. What good would it do anyway?

To my total amazement, that was pretty much how my day went. It was like my old dream had finally come true—like I was the most popular girl in school and everyone loved me. Too weird. Everyone kept coming up and showing their support for me. And yet with each time, I felt more and more miserable. But how could I explain this to anyone? I didn't even get it myself. And I'm sure that everyone thought they were just being nice. And they were—to *me* anyway. But the nasty things they were saying about Shawna were almost making me feel sick.

Even Brett, with Ashley at his side, came to talk to me during lunch. "Looks like we've been cleared, Jordan."

I smiled up at him. "That was pretty weird, huh?"

"You're telling me. I thought someone was going to pop out with a camera and say, 'You've been had, Brett Hawkins, you're on *Gotcha TV!*'"

I laughed. "Yeah, I honestly thought we'd slipped into an old episode of *The Twilight Zone.*"

"I'm just glad it's over," said Ashley. "What a nightmare."

"How's your foot?" asked Brett.

"Okay, considering."

"Was your car totaled?"

I nodded.

"Bummer," said Ashley.

"You could probably sue Shawna," said Brett. "It's really her fault that you got into that wreck."

"Maybe. But it was my choice to go." I don't know if it was God or just me, but I felt a need to say something more honest. "And in all fairness, at the time I really did think I was going to see Timothy, even though I knew he was still going with Shawna."

"Yeah, sure, but considering everything," said Ashley, "it's pretty hard to feel sorry for *her.*"

"Yeah, she totally set you up," said Brett. "And me too. I think that girl deserves whatever she gets."

"Amber said she might get kicked off the squad," said Ashley.

"Good," said Brett. "We don't need someone like Shawna Frye dragging us all down during basketball season, especially when it looks like we might really have a chance at state."

Then, to my relief, the subject moved on to basketball. But I was still thinking about Shawna. And to my amazement, I no longer felt like I wanted to make her miserable. It's not like I wanted to be friends with her or anything, and I had no problem that kids were siding with me instead of her, but that old seething hatred I'd carried all those weeks seemed to be melting away.

At the end of fifth period, I received a memo from Ms. Brookes informing me that my probation period had ended. She wanted me to come talk to her before my next class.

"I'm really sorry about that day in the parking lot," I told her after I thanked her for the memo. "I don't usually talk like that."

"I know." She smiled. "Amber told me about the stolen car keys and jeans." She shook her head. "Not exactly the behavior we expect from our girls."

"Love does strange things to people," I said and then I wished I hadn't, since now she was looking at me like I was slightly nuts.

"So, how long will you be in that cast?" she asked.

"Until early January," I told her. "Almost half of basketball season."

She shook her head. "We're going to have to call in the alternate."

I nodded. "Yeah, I figured you would. If she's my size, I'd be happy to give her my outfits."

Ms. Brookes laughed. "First of all, she's not even close to your size. But second of all, you're still on the squad, Jordan—unless you're thinking of quitting."

"Huh?"

"Pardon me," she corrected.

"Right. Pardon me?"

"No, Shawna's the one who's being dismissed."

"Oh."

She peered closely at me. "Do you have a problem with that, Jordan?"

"I guess I feel a little sorry for her."

"Well, that's nice and all. But she's broken too many of the rules to even be considered for a simple probation. We don't have you girls sign that pledge just for the fun of it, you know."

"I know."

"And we expect you to attend practices. You don't have to work out; just be there. And dress in uniform on game days, and, well, just do whatever you can do to boost morale. They'll need it."

I nodded. "Of course. I'll do whatever I can. And maybe I'll get out of the cast sooner—"

"Don't be rushing things, Jordan. Just get that foot healed up right."

"Okay."

"I'll be announcing this to the rest of the girls today. Do you know if Shawna's shown up yet?"

"I haven't seen her."

She shook her head. "Unfortunately, it seems that Shawna is skipping school today—another infraction. I've already spoken to her mother about her being suspended from the squad, but I can't seem to reach Shawna on her cell or at home. I really wanted her to hear the news from me first, but we need to get our alternate on board and practicing if we're going to have the slightest chance at Flair Fair."

I nodded, but I had to wonder if Flair Fair was becoming a little too important, not just to the cheerleaders but to Ms. Brookes as well. Still, I was the newcomer here, and not exactly an asset when it came to the competition anyway.

We were a somber group as we met in Ms. Brookes' office after school. At first I wondered why Lucy Farrell was there, but then I figured she must be the alternate. I felt bad for everyone when we were all subjected to a rather lengthy and somewhat boring lecture on (1) propriety, (2) respect, (3) rules, and (4) leadership.

"And this is exactly why Shawna Frye is officially suspended as a cheerleader starting today. I have spent the day trying to reach her, and her mother has been informed. But it's time to move on, and since Lucy Farrell was the first alternate, we can all welcome her to the squad today."

"You mean Shawna hasn't even been told yet?" demanded Betsy Mosler.

"Excuse me, Betsy," said Ms. Brookes in a firm voice. "We were about to welcome Lucy to the squad."

Amber started clapping and we all followed suit, but Betsy was scowling. She raised her hand and asked her question again.

"As I said, her mother has been notified." Ms. Brookes sighed. "There's little I can do when a cheerleader breaks the rules and then skips school and cannot be reached. I hope this will be a lesson to all of us. You girls are the leaders in this school. We expect more of you."

By the time she finished her speech, my foot was really throbbing and all I wanted to do was to go home and crash. But then I remembered that I was supposed to stay "for all practices." I considered pleading my case and then thought better of it. Instead, I tried to make myself comfortable on the bleachers and somehow managed to crank out quite a bit of homework while trying to look somewhat attentive to the practice. I had to feel sorry for Lucy though. It seemed like she was getting the brunt of all the pent-up frustration of the squad. And Betsy, in particular, had really focused her sights on the poor girl.

"Lucy is *never* going to get it," complained Betsy as they were finishing up. "We'd be better off without her."

"Sure, a squad with only five girls," said Ashley sarcastically.

"It's times like this I wish we still had the guys around," said Amber as she wiped her face with a towel.

"I don't see why they quit having guys on the team," said Jenny.

Ashley glanced over her shoulder first to make sure it was safe before she spoke. "I think it was Ms. Brookes' suggestion," she said. "She thought that inappropriate lifting was going on."

"Lifting?" I called as I hobbled over toward them.

"You know," said Ashley. "The guys were getting too friendly when they lifted the girls into the air."

We all laughed—well, everyone but Lucy.

"Don't worry, Lucy," I said quietly as we headed toward the locker room. "It's always hardest at the beginning."

"I was so excited earlier today," she told me. "Now I feel like a complete failure. And tomorrow's the first preseason game."

"You'll be fine. Just take a spot on the end and step aside

whenever you forget. Believe me, that's better than standing out there looking stupid."

"Thanks." She smiled at me and then looked down at my foot. "Bet that hurt."

I nodded. "And it's not feeling too hot right now either."

"You need a ride home, Jordan?" called Ashley as she headed for the showers.

"That'd be great."

On the way home, Ashley asked me if I was still interested in working at her mom's shop.

"I would be," I told her, "but I'm such a klutz, I'd probably end up knocking everything over."

"Yeah, better wait. Hey!" Suddenly she was pulling her car to a stop. "That's Shawna's car!"

Sure enough, it *was* Shawna's car. "Are you going to talk to her?"

"Why not?" said Ashley as she pulled into the convenience-store parking lot, parking right next to Shawna's car. "Someone has to tell her the good news."

I frowned, unsure this was such a good idea. "Maybe Amber—"

"Come on, Jordan. You should totally enjoy this!"

"Oh, Ashley, my foot is really hurting right now. All I want to do is take a pain pill and go to sleep."

"Yeah, yeah, okay. But I'll put the windows down so you can hear her reaction."

I cringed. This was not going to be pretty.

Ashley leaned back on the hood of her own car, waiting for Shawna to come out. Finally, Shawna emerged carrying a large drink and what looked like a hot dog. I couldn't believe Shawna would actually eat a convenience-store hot dog.

"Hey, Shawna," called Ashley.

I slunk down in the seat of her car, out of Shawna's view, wishing I weren't there at all.

"What's up?" asked Shawna in a flat tone.

"Have you heard the news?"

Shawna's brows lifted slightly. She'd been hooked. "No, what news?"

"*Well,*" Ashley drawled as if the word had three syllables. "Ms. Brookes put Lucy Farrell on the squad today."

Now Shawna visibly brightened. *"Really?"* She took a sip of her drink. "So is that backstabbing little tramp history now?"

I saw Ashley glance over to where I was sitting, and Shawna's gaze quickly followed, but I was already out of the car. Sore foot or not, I wasn't going to take that kind of abuse sitting down.

"Did you have something to say to *me?*" I hobbled over to stand next to Ashley, hoping she'd protect me if Shawna got out of hand. Not that she would. Shawna may be a lot of things, but she's not a physical bully.

Shawna just tossed me a look that suggested I wasn't worthy of her attention. "Too bad, Jordan. But with your messed up foot and all, you shouldn't have expected to remain on the squad. It's not like we can afford to have cripples out there leading cheers."

"Lucy isn't replacing Jordan," said Ashley.

Shawna's eyes narrowed. "What do you mean?"

"She's replacing *you.*"

"Yeah, I'm sure."

"Ms. Brookes has been trying to reach you all day, Shawna. She finally got your mom at work."

"Are you serious?" Shawna looked stressed now.

Ashley just nodded.

Then Shawna used a word that Ms. Brookes would not have approved of, jumped in her car, and squealed out of the parking lot.

Ashley just shrugged. "Well, at least she knows."

I rolled my eyes. "Can we go home now?"

If all this had happened a few weeks ago, or even a week ago, I would've been ecstatic — over the moon with joy. But today I just felt tired and slightly confused.

After a quiet dinner with my family, I called Kara.

"How are you doing?" she asked in a cheerful voice.

"I'm not sure."

"I tried to hook up with you at school, but every time I saw you, you were surrounded by friends. It's like you were some kind of celebrity or something today. What's up?"

"Didn't Edgar tell you?"

She laughed. "Well, he told me that Amber had been setting everyone straight about what really happened."

"Which reminds me," I said. "How did the truth first start coming to the surface, Kara? When Amber came to my house, she had already heard the rumor."

"Well, it's not really like spreading a rumor when you're telling the truth," said Kara. "Edgar just happened to tell the truth to the right people, and it took off like any other sort of rumor."

"I owe him one."

"Yeah, me too. But what's going on with you today? You sound kind of bummed."

"I think I'm a little dazed and confused."

So I told her about my mixed feelings for Shawna and how I didn't want to let God down by acting like a jerk.

"That's because you need to forgive her," said Kara as if that should make perfect sense.

"Forgive her?" I repeated. "Forgive Shawna?"

"Yeah."

"After all the crud she's put me through? Even today. You should've heard what she said to me at the store, Kara. It was bad."

"I'm sure it was. She probably hates your guts, considering all that's gone down."

"But it was *her* fault." I knew I sounded just like my friends now.

"I'm sure it was," agreed Kara. "That's not the point."

"What *is* the point?"

Kara sighed. "I know this is a lot for you to take in, Jordan. I mean, you only gave your heart to God yesterday. But just bear with me, okay?"

"Okay." I leaned back on my bed, perching my cast-bound foot on a pillow.

"Well, the thing is, Jesus forgives us, right?"

"Right," I said. "He cleans up our messes like Little Cat Z."

"Yeah, right. I can see I'm going to have to read that book."

"I think Tommy's still got a copy," I teased. "I'll bet he'd loan it to you."

"Thanks. Anyway, in the same way that Jesus forgives us—while we're total messes—that's how he wants us to forgive other people too."

"Oh." Now, to be honest, this struck a familiar chord, like maybe I'd heard this same thing in church one time, although I usually never paid too much attention in church.

"Yeah. And it's not easy. Remember what I told you the other day about Bree?"

"Yeah."

"Well, today she made off with my Doc Marten boots."

"Are her feet your size now?"

"Apparently." Kara's voice sounded a bit strained. "So, even as I'm telling you that you need to forgive Shawna, I'm wanting to strangle my little sister. And she's my own flesh and blood, for crying out loud."

"So what are you going to do?"

"I guess I'll have to ask God to help me."

"Oh."

"That's probably what you should do too, Jordan."

"But what if it doesn't work? Like, what will you do if Bree keeps taking your clothes?"

"I'm not sure. I keep imagining all of my clothes disappearing from my closet and showing up in Bree's. I'll probably end up going to school wearing a sheet someday."

"Everyone would probably think you'd joined a cult," I teased.

"Maybe that's how those kinds of things get started in the first place."

We both laughed and then said goodbye.

I actually considered getting down on my knees right then, thinking perhaps that was the proper way to pray, but my foot was really throbbing.

"Do you mind if I pray flat on my back, God?" I began. And I didn't get the impression that he minded, so I continued.

First I asked him to help me become a better person, and then I asked him to help me forgive Shawna. I admitted that I didn't really feel like forgiving her, but I didn't want to make any more messes either.

Before I could say "amen," I had fallen asleep. Somehow I don't think God minded that either.

twenty-two

"ISN'T IT GREAT THAT LUCY IS ALMOST THE SAME SIZE AS SHAWNA?" asked Jenny as we gathered at the foot of the bleachers before the first basketball game of the season. Lucy had on Shawna's old uniform along with an enormous smile. I could sense her excitement about being the newest member of the squad. I remembered how I'd once felt like that. Had it only been a few months ago?

Respecting Ms. Brookes' policy, I was also wearing my uniform, although I felt a little awkward and out of place with my giant "club foot," as Ashley had taken to calling it. But the girls had wrapped stripes of red and blue crepe paper around my crutches, complete with these funky miniature pom-poms tied to the sides. I didn't feel too bad about hanging out on the sidelines tonight.

"I'd like to know how Ms. Brookes got Shawna to give up her uniform," I said, glancing nervously around the gym that was slowly filling up. I wondered if Shawna would show up, or if she did, whether she might pull some kind of revenge stunt. I'd started watching my backside after what she'd said the other day in the parking lot.

"Yeah," said Ashley. "I can just imagine Shawna saying, 'Oh, sure, you can have my uniform, but not until you pry it out of my cold dead hands.'"

Everyone laughed.

Lucy wasn't doing too badly, considering she'd only been to two practices so far. And it seemed she was taking my advice about staying on the end of the line and stepping out and just clapping and smiling when she didn't quite remember the routine. I felt sorry for her but knew she'd get the hang of it before too long.

In a way, I think I almost enjoyed being slightly incapacitated, since it allowed me to relax a little and actually focus on the basketball game—or, more accurately, on Timothy.

He had finally spoken to me today. It was toward the end of lunch when he came over and asked me if I could use some help putting away my tray. Ashley winked at me, as if to say, "Go girl," and I accepted his offer.

"I've been wanting to talk to you, Jordan," he said as he dumped the tray onto the heap. "Got a minute?"

I nodded and followed his lead to a table on the perimeter of the cafeteria.

"How's your foot?" he asked with a concerned look.

"It's not hurting too much right now."

"That's good."

We sat down on either side of a small table, and I just looked at him. He seemed slightly stressed.

"How're you doing?" I asked.

He shrugged but said nothing, and we both just sat there in silence for a couple of very long seconds.

Finally I couldn't take it. "Hey, I thought you wanted to talk to me."

The corners of his lips curved up into what was almost a smile. "Yeah. Sorry. Mostly I just wanted to tell you that I'm sorry for acting like such a total jerk with you these last few weeks."

Now *I* shrugged. "Hey, we've all been acting pretty lame lately."

"I guess. But I also wanted to tell you that I am totally finished with Shawna. I don't even know why I stayed with her as long as I did. Our relationship was pretty messed up."

I nodded.

"And I guess I was just hoping that you and I could be, well, maybe we could be friends again, Jordan. I know you've been through a lot and you probably need some time to think about this. But I really do like you. You're fun to be with and you're easy to talk to. I think about you a lot. And, well, it seems like we never really got a fair shot at being together. I can see now how Shawna was always messing with us."

"She didn't want to let you go." I frowned. "She may not want to let you go now."

He nodded. "Yeah, that's probably true. But I am cutting her off completely, cold turkey. Believe me, I have absolutely no interest in that girl, especially after the moronic stunt she pulled with you and Brett last week. I mean, how low did she plan to go?"

"Do you think she'll do anything else?"

"I don't see the point. I told her in no uncertain terms that we were finished, history, done."

"That's probably good."

"Yeah. I'd rather not have a girlfriend at all than have someone like her. She was making me crazy with her pranks, not to mention how it's been hurting my game. And I really need to stay focused right now, Jordan. There's a chance I might pick up a small scholarship if the team goes to state this year."

"That's cool."

He smiled now. "And you seem like the kind of girl who gets that, like you'd be supportive of me and not mess with my mind all the time."

I smiled, a familiar warm rush running through me. "Yeah. I think you're a great ball player, Timothy. In fact, I'm really looking forward to seeing you play tonight."

His eyes brightened. "Really?"

"Oh, yeah!"

"Cool." Then he reached across the table as if to take my hand, but then we simply shook like we'd reached some sort of business agreement. "Friends?" he asked with his charming smile.

"You bet."

Of course, I knew that he was probably thinking more than just "friends," but I appreciated his willingness to take this thing slowly. After everything that had transpired this fall, it felt like we all needed a little breather. And I can totally understand his need to stay focused on his game too. But as I stood at the foot of the bleachers, playing the crippled but enthusiastic cheerleader, I stayed focused on him.

Not only did we win our game but Timothy scored twenty-eight points, and we solidly whupped Franklin 53–40. I cheered so loudly that I was slightly hoarse by the time we all went out for pizza to celebrate our first victory of the season.

"You need a ride home?" Timothy asked me as the party started breaking up.

I'd come with Ashley but overheard her offering Brett a ride home and figured she'd probably appreciate it if I caught a ride with someone else. "Sure," I told him. "I'll let Ashley know."

I saw her brows lift as I told her. "See," she said, "I told you it was just a matter of time before you two were back together."

"We're not back together," I told her. "We're just friends and he's just giving me a ride."

"Yeah, whatever." She winked at me. "Don't do anything I wouldn't do."

I rolled my eyes at her and held up a crutch as if to remind her that she was talking to a poor crippled girl now. "Yeah, you bet."

We mostly talked about the game as we rode home, but Timothy turned off the engine when he got to my house. He turned around in his seat to face me. Then, playing with my hair, he told me that he still remembered that day when his dad caught us at the park.

I felt my cheeks growing warm and was glad it was dark enough that he couldn't see I was embarrassed. "Well, that'd be pretty hard to reenact," I told him lightly. "I mean, with this cast on my foot and all." I laughed. "I can't see myself climbing in and out of your backseat."

He laughed too. "No, I wasn't suggesting that." Then he leaned toward me for a kiss. I leaned toward him, and soon we were kissing. And even though it felt good to have his lips pressed against mine, I felt something else too—uncomfortable. Finally, I pushed him away and caught my breath.

"What's wrong?" he asked.

I didn't know what to say. "It's my stupid foot," I told him. "It's really starting to throb." Now this wasn't untrue, but that wasn't what was actually bothering me either.

"Oh," he said, and I could sense the disappointment in his voice. "You should probably go inside, huh?"

"Yeah, probably."

"I wanted to ask you something first, Jordie."

"Sure. What?"

"Do you think you'd like to go to the Winter Dance with me next Saturday?"

I smiled and then remembered my foot. "Well, I wouldn't be much good on the dance floor."

"That's okay. I'm not that crazy about dancing anyway." He

grinned. "Your foot will give me the perfect excuse to just sit around and hang out."

"Okay," I told him. "That sounds like fun."

"Cool."

Then he went around and opened the door and helped me out of the car. I've noticed that his manners have improved since I broke my foot. He used to just let me climb out of the car on my own. Then he walked me to the front door and kissed me again. Not just a goodnight peck either. He was kissing me so intently that he didn't even seem to notice when the window shade lifted slightly and someone in my family peeked at us.

"I need to go inside," I told him as I pushed him away. "Goodnight."

He nodded. "Yeah. See ya."

Thankfully it was only Leah playing spy tonight. "Hot date?" she asked as I made my way inside.

"Yeah, thanks for being such a snoop," I told her.

"Well, I thought it might've been a burglar, and Mom and Dad already went to bed."

"Yeah, sure."

"Cute crutches." She flipped one of the pom-poms.

"Thanks." I dropped my bag on a chair.

"Need any help getting upstairs?"

"Thanks, but I can handle it." I'd gotten pretty good at going up and down stairs on crutches.

"Are you okay, Jordan?"

I turned and looked at her. "Huh?"

"I don't know, you just seem different. Kind of bummed or something."

I shook my head. "I think I'm just tired."

"Oh."

So I slowly made my way upstairs and finally, alone in my room, flopped down across my bed and wondered what was bugging me. It was kind of like that Little Cat Z thing again. Not a voice exactly but just this feeling that something was wrong.

"What is it?" I wondered. Then I prayed that if God was really trying to tell me something, I'd be able to hear him and understand it. But nothing really seemed to be coming to me, although I did suspect that it had to do with Timothy. Still, I felt too exhausted to figure it out tonight. Maybe God would help me to figure it out tomorrow. It took all the energy I had just to get out of my uniform and ready for bed. But before I went to sleep I prayed and asked God to show me what it was that he wanted me to do about Timothy.

On one hand, I thought it was kind of cool that Timothy and I were finally getting together—for real this time. And I wondered if perhaps God had done that for me. But on the other hand, I felt a little uneasy about the whole thing. Part of me felt like I couldn't really trust Timothy. But I didn't know where that was coming from.

twenty-three

KARA DROPPED BY THE NEXT MORNING. I'D BEEN FEELING KIND OF BAD that I hadn't talked to her much lately, especially after how great she and Edgar had been after my accident.

"What's up?" I asked when she unexpectedly popped into the kitchen, where I was slowly munching down a bowl of Frosted Flakes.

"I was just out riding my bike and thought I'd stop in and say hi," she told me. "Your mom was loading some stuff into her truck and said to just let myself in."

"Want some?" I held up the cereal box.

She grinned. "Sure."

"You know where to find things," I said, remembering how she practically used to live at my house, back when we'd been best friends.

"So how's it going?" she asked as she sat down with her bowl of cereal.

Even though she's not much of a sports enthusiast, I filled her in on last night's victory. "It was a great way to start the season."

"Cool."

"And then Timothy brought me home," I said, kind of just leaving that statement to hang in the air. I'm not even sure why.

"Oh." She looked slightly troubled by this.

"And he invited me to the Winter Dance."

"Oh."

"That's all you can say, Kara?" I studied her closely. "Oh?"

"Well."

"Oh and well." I shook my head. "Quite the little conversationalist."

"What do you want me to say?" She put a spoonful of cereal in her mouth.

"I don't know."

She swallowed. "What do you think of it?"

"Of what?"

"Of you and Timothy getting back together."

I frowned. "I'm not really sure."

"Uh-huh?"

"I mean, it's kind of cool and everything. But at the same time—oh, I don't know."

"But at the same time what?"

"Well, maybe something doesn't feel quite right or the same as before. But I don't even know what."

"Maybe getting Timothy isn't such a big deal when it's not a contest with Shawna."

"I don't think that's it."

She shrugged. "Maybe God is trying to tell you something."

"I actually wondered about that last night. But what?"

"Maybe Timothy isn't the right guy for you."

"What do you mean?"

"You probably know what I mean, Jordan."

I glanced around to make sure that none of my family members were within earshot then spoke quietly. "You mean sex?"

She nodded. "Seems like it was an issue with you guys."

"An issue?"

"You know, with Shawna using it to get him back from you, and then you were going to use it to get him back from Shawna."

"So, what are you saying?"

"Maybe God is trying to warn you or something."

"But I don't plan on having"—I lowered my voice again—"sex."

"But maybe Timothy does."

I laughed and held up my cast-encased foot. "Yeah, I can just see us getting it on with this thing."

"You're not going to be wearing that forever. Besides, I'm sure that it's possible to have sex with a broken bone. You could call and ask your doctor."

"Oh, sure. Hand me the phone, will you?"

She laughed but then got serious. "But really, Jordan, you have to know that it's going to be a pretty big issue with Timothy."

I sighed. "Maybe so. But I just don't want to think about that right now."

"Fine. You're the one who brought it up." She smiled. "Thanks for the cereal."

"You going to eat and run?"

"Actually, I have to babysit for my neighbor this afternoon. I should get back." Then she paused. "Oh, yeah, I almost forgot. Edgar told me to invite you to youth group tonight."

"Edgar *told* you?"

"Well, I happen to think it's a good idea too. I mean, I realize you have your own church and everything, but Edgar thought you might like to visit just for the fun of it. Our youth pastor is pretty cool."

So that's how I ended up at Edgar Peebles' youth group on a Saturday night. It was kind of weird, because I felt a little embarrassed to be there, and yet I felt really comfortable too, like it was the first time I'd been with a group of kids and able to just relax and be myself. And the kids were this strange mix. Geeks and freaks and nerds and academics and jocks, but most surprising of all was Lucy Farrell.

"I didn't know you were a Christian," she said to me.

"Same back at you."

She grinned. "I guess it's not the kind of thing you go around announcing over the PA system at school."

"I've been a Christian for only a few days," I admitted, "so this is all pretty new to me."

"Well, this is a cool group." She smiled at Kara and Edgar. "Good to see you guys."

So I was starting to feel like maybe this wasn't going to be so bad. But then the youth pastor dude started to talk, and when he announced that the topic of the evening was about forgiving your enemies, I wanted to bolt right out the door. It was like I knew he was talking directly to me—about Shawna. I even wondered if Edgar or Kara had actually tipped him off.

I tried not to listen too carefully, but this guy had a way of saying things that got under my skin. And before long, I realized that he totally made sense. It was just like Kara had been trying to tell me: How can you expect God to forgive you if you can't forgive someone else?

"The cool thing about this kind of forgiveness," he finally said, "is that you can't even begin to do it without God's help. He's the only one who can show us how to forgive like this. And if you try to do it on your own, it'll just turn into a mess." And then we prayed.

He asked God to guide us in forgiving others. Then he said "amen" and that was it.

"Did you tell him about me?" I whispered to Kara as we made our way to the snack table.

"Huh?"

"Did you tell your youth pastor about how I need to forgive Shawna?"

She laughed. "Oh, sure. I called him up and asked him to talk about this just for you." She shook her head. "Give God some credit, Jordan."

I smiled a little sheepishly. "Okay. Sorry to sound so paranoid."

"It's okay. I remember feeling like that too. It's like God starts to nail you on something and you just don't get how he can do it so efficiently."

"I guess."

So I came home tonight and wondered just how I was supposed to handle this thing with Shawna. I mean, how does a person go about forgiving another person? Do you call her up on the phone? Write a letter or email? Go in person? Or is it just between you and God? I wasn't sure. And so I prayed again and asked God to show me. But to be perfectly honest, I was hoping he wouldn't show me anytime soon. I didn't really think I was quite ready for this.

The following day, probably due to the fact that I'd gone to youth group the night before, my mom decided we should all go to church together.

"But we hardly ever go," said Leah as we all piled into the car. "What's so special about today?"

"It'll make it easier when we go at Christmas," said my mom. "It won't seem so much like we're the kind of people who only go on the holidays."

"But we *are* those kind of people," complained Leah.

"It can't be *that* bad," I said to Leah.

Dad winked at me as he closed the car door.

And I suppose it wasn't. But I could hardly believe my ears when Pastor Griswold also started preaching about forgiveness. Like don't these pastors have anything else to talk about? Or had they gotten together and synchronized their messages specially for me this week? Anyway, Pastor Griswold said that nothing makes God feel worse than when we refuse to forgive someone after God has forgiven us. He also said how forgiveness is usually a two-way street. Often we need to ask people to forgive us as much as we need to forgive them. And to be perfectly honest, I knew that I had done Shawna wrong too. But the idea of asking her to forgive me felt pretty overwhelming. I wondered if it would be okay to just tell her I was sorry. At least it would be a step in the right direction. So when I got home after church, I went to my room and asked God to help me figure this thing out.

Although I felt like I needed to take care of it, and as soon as possible, I still wasn't quite sure how to go about it. Like, I couldn't see myself having my mom drive me over to Shawna's and then hobbling up to her door and telling her that I was sorry. I mean, I want to obey God and everything, but how lame would that be? And an email seemed slightly impersonal. Plus, I remembered how she had used email in her little setup. Finally, it seemed that a phone call was the best route. I prayed as I dialed her number and then felt my hands actually shaking as I listened to the phone ring. I seriously hoped she wasn't home and even considered hanging up before the message machine came on, except that I know she has caller ID.

"Hello?"

I thought it was Shawna, although her voice sounded flat and tired and totally unlike the old Shawna.

"Shawna?"

"Yeah."

I took a breath. "This is Jordan."

No response.

"I want to talk to you about something."

Still no response. Had she hung up?

"Do you have a minute?"

"Depends."

"On what?"

"What do you *want*, Jordan?" Her voice was seriously irritated now, and I half expected her to hang up on me.

"Well, it's kind of a long story." I paused to see if she had a problem with that, but when she said nothing, I continued. "I realize there's a lot of crud between us and everything. And first of all, I want to tell you I'm sorry for some things I said and did to you, mostly in regard to Timothy."

"Whatever." She sounded bored now.

"And, well, I became a Christian recently and—"

"Are you for *real*?"

"Huh?"

"What's up with you, Jordan? Why are you calling me like this?"

"Like I said, I invited God into my life and I know that he wants me to make things right with you, or at least try. And I just wanted to tell you that I'm sorry and that I'm not going to hold any of this against you. That's all."

Dead silence.

"Are you still there?"

"Yeah. But why are you saying that?"

"What?"

"That you're not going to hold this against me? I mean, it doesn't make sense. Why aren't you totally ticked off at me, Jordan?"

"Because of God. I realized that I needed to tell you I was sorry and that I'm not carrying a grudge. I just thought I should let you know."

"Why?"

"I don't know exactly why." I thought hard about what Pastor Griswold had said this morning. "I guess it's just because that's what God wants us to do. He forgives us and we're supposed to forgive others. It's really pretty simple."

"So are you serious, Jordan?" Her voice had softened just a little. "No hard feelings?"

"Yes. Totally."

"So, what's the deal then? Do you expect something from me?"

"No, I just wanted to let you know."

"And do you, like, think this means we're going to be good friends again?" I could hear the distinct note of sarcasm in her voice.

"No, that's not it. I just hope we won't hate each other anymore."

"Yeah, I'll bet you do."

"Look, it's your choice, Shawna. But for the record, I don't hate you anymore."

"Whatever."

"And I'm really sorry that everything got so messed up for you lately."

"Yeah, I'll just bet you are." Now that old sharp edge returned to her voice. "Betsy already told me that you and Timothy are back together—"

"We're not really back together again."

"Yeah, sure, whatever."

"Really. We've talked and stuff. And he asked me to the Winter Dance. But I'm not even sure that's what I want anymore." I couldn't believe that I was actually confessing this to Shawna Frye, of all people. I mean, who knew what she might do with something like this?

Now she laughed. But it was a harsh, bitter-sounding laugh.

"Really, Shawna, the only reason I called was to say I'm sorry. And I hope you're doing okay."

"So, you're really serious about this God thing?"

"Yeah."

"It's not just some cheap little trick for getting back at me?"

"Honestly, Shawna. I gave my heart to God and I'm trying to live my life differently."

"Jordan Ferguson gets religion." It sounded like the title of a TV movie.

"Yeah, something like that." I really wanted to end this conversation now.

"Well, that's pretty weird."

I sighed. "Yeah, I'm sure it seems weird to you. And it did to me at first, but it makes more sense every day."

"And you really aren't getting back together with Timothy?"

I considered this before I gave her my most truthful answer. "The more I think about it, the more I feel pretty certain that I'm not."

"Well, it just figures."

"What?"

She didn't say anything.

"So, really, Shawna, if you think you and Timothy still have something, seriously, I *won't* be standing in your way anymore."

Now she laughed again. But her laughter seemed worn out and perhaps laced with sadness. "Oh, you got that right, Jordan. Timothy and I still *do* have something."

I blinked in surprise, since Timothy had sounded like they were totally over. "Well, hey, that's cool with me. Really."

"Yeah, I'm sure it is. I wasn't even going to tell you either."

"You don't have—"

"No, why not? Why not just lay all the cards on the table, Jordan. In case you're interested, that special something that Timothy and I *have* together"—she paused—"is something you'll be just as glad not to get."

"Huh?"

"Timothy infected me with an STD."

"STD?" I knew I'd heard those initials before, but it took me a split second to realize that she was actually talking about a sexually transmitted disease. "Are you serious?"

"I got the freaking results back from the doctor on Friday."

"Oh, man, I am so sorry, Shawna."

"Yeah, me too. And maybe I'm just assuming something here . . ." Then she paused again. "Or maybe I'm wrong, but the last I heard, you and Timothy hadn't actually done it or else you'd better get yourself checked too."

"Oh, no problem, I don't need to get checked." I felt a new rush of relief.

"Lucky you." But her voice sounded flat and tired again.

"Have you told Timothy yet?"

"I called him yesterday and he accused me of making the whole thing up."

"But you're not, are you?"

"Yeah, right." She sighed. "Sheesh, why would I make up something like this, Jordan? It's not like it makes me look good. But, hey, if you don't believe me, you could always go ahead and find out for yourself."

"Yeah, thanks a lot."

"Don't mention it."

"I hope you're getting good treatment for it, Shawna."

"Oh, it's the best that modern medicine has to offer. It can control the symptoms, but the disease will be with me until someone invents a cure, which might not be for a few more decades."

"I really am sorry."

"Yeah, me too."

"Take care."

"Thanks. And thanks for calling."

I hung up the phone and just shook my head. *An STD?* That was just too much to even begin to wrap my head around. All I could do was pray. First I thanked God for protecting me, and then I prayed for both Shawna and Timothy. I wasn't even sure *how* I should pray for them. But mostly, I just asked God to help them come to him in the same way that I was coming to him. "They're going to need you," I prayed. "Please help them find you."

twenty-four

SOMEHOW, AND I SUPPOSE IT'S NOT TERRIBLY SURPRISING, THE WORD GOT out that Shawna and Timothy both have an STD. Thankfully, I was *not* the informant. And also thankfully, I had already broken things off with Tim before this became common knowledge.

"I really don't think I'm ready for a relationship right now," I had told him last Monday. "You see, I just gave my heart to God and there are a few things I need to figure out right now. And consequently, I can't go to the dance with you either."

I wasn't that surprised when he barely reacted to my gentle rejection. He obviously had bigger problems on his mind now, and it was hard not to feel sorry for him.

It was toward the middle of the week that the rumor really began circulating. I think it actually started out among the guys. Who says guys don't gossip? But then on Friday a new story began spreading like wildfire.

"Did you hear the latest?" Jenny pulled me aside right before second period. She had this total look of horror in her eyes.

"What's wrong?" I asked, certain there must be a student with a machine gun holding half the students hostage somewhere.

"Timothy has to quit basketball!"

"Oh. I thought it was something *really* serious."

"This *is* serious," she said. "Now there's no way we can go to state this year."

"Why is he quitting?" I asked.

"They say it's because of the treatment he's taking for the STD. He's allergic to penicillin, so they have to do some kind of experimental drug that might cause him to have a heart attack if he's playing basketball."

"No, really?"

"Really. Not only is he out of luck with the ladies but now he doesn't even have sports to fall back on."

"I guess this wipes out all hope of a scholarship too." I shook my head. "He must be feeling rotten."

And I'm sure it doesn't help that all of his friends are pretty mad at him now, like he personally decided to ruin this basketball season for everyone.

"I can't believe he did this to us," said Ashley as we stood in the lunch line.

"Did this to *us?*" I echoed. "What about *him?*"

"He's getting what he deserves," she said as she picked up a salad. "It's just not fair that he has to drag the whole school down with him."

"Well, according to what I read last night, he's not the only one with this kind of problem." Now, I hate to admit that I had gotten a little worried about all this STD business myself. I mean, I realize we'd only kissed, but I wasn't totally sure that these viruses were *only* transmitted through the actual sexual deed. Just to be safe, I decided to do a little research.

"What do you mean?" Ashley frowned at me.

"I mean, according to statistics, Shawna and Timothy can't be the only ones at school with an STD. There are probably a whole bunch of other kids who should get checked, whether they have symptoms or not."

"Well, thanks for making my day," said Ashley.

"Hey, don't shoot the messenger. This is probably something they covered in health class anyway."

"Like we ever listened." Ashley rolled her eyes.

So everyone was in a pretty foul mood at school today. Ironically enough, we had a pep assembly this afternoon and, let me tell you, it was totally pathetic. Not only was it poorly attended but the kids who did show up had about as much enthusiasm as a pile of turnips. I was actually glad that I didn't have to be down on the gym floor with the rest of the cheerleaders, trying to generate some lukewarm enthusiasm. It's really amazing how everything can change in the course of a week.

But here's something that happened that kind of made my day. Shawna actually came up to talk to me after the assembly.

"I've been thinking about what you said, Jordan, and I just wanted to apologize to you for all the crud I pulled. I'm sorry."

Now call me skeptical or just slightly paranoid, but at first I wasn't totally sure that this wasn't just another one of her tricks. But when I looked into her eyes, I could see them getting watery and I could tell she was about to cry.

"Thanks," I told her. "I appreciate that. And, really, I'm sorry too."

"This really blows, you know." She shook her head and watched as the somber crowd exited the gym.

"Yeah, I know. I feel bad for both you and Timothy."

"I'm actually starting to feel a little bit sorry for Timothy myself—well, when I'm not consumed with anger, that is."

"I'm sure he's pretty bummed."

"Well, I'll bet you're feeling pretty lucky, eh? Like you missed a bullet?"

"I'm mostly just thankful to God. I think he was watching over me."

"Nice that he watches over *some* of us." I could hear the cut in her voice.

"Well, I was asking for his help," I explained. "It's not like he's going to force anyone to do anything. You have to be willing, you know."

"Actually, I *don't* know."

"Well, maybe you'd like to hear more about it sometime."

She seemed to consider this. "Yeah, maybe." Then she walked off, and I heard Ashley yelling at me to hurry up if I wanted a ride home.

"Go on without me," I called out to her. "I'm getting a ride with Kara."

She stopped and looked at me like I had just announced that I was catching the next UFO shuttle to Jupiter. "What?"

"I'm getting a ride with Kara Hendricks."

She walked up and looked at me like I had an eyeball hanging out of its socket. "You mean Kara, the art freak, Hendricks?"

I nodded. "Actually, Edgar Peebles is driving. We're going out for coffee."

"Man, first the whole freaking school is falling apart and now you're flipping out on us too, Ferguson." She sadly shook her head as she walked away, probably on her way to let my other so-called friends know that I was losing it. But at least Lucy would get it.

I had a great visit with Kara and Edgar at Jitters. Edgar announced that Timothy Lawrence now holds the number-one position on his prayer list.

"Who'd you have to bump?" I asked.

He pointed his finger in my direction.

"Oh."

"But don't worry, I'll still be praying for you." He smiled. "I pray for all my friends."

"Well, if your prayers for Timothy are as successful as they were for me, he'll be in good hands."

Because that's just how it feels to me, like my life is finally in good hands. I cringe to remember what a mess I made of my life, all for the love of a boy. Or at least what I *thought* was love. Now I'm not so sure what it was. Maybe it was infatuation or delusion or perhaps even my old obsessive-compulsive nature. Or maybe it was just plain and simple jealousy. Whatever it was, I'm thankful that it's over and that I won't be going back there again.

reader's guide

1. Jordan begins dating Timothy immediately after he breaks up with her best friend, Shawna. Do you think this was okay? Why or why not?

2. Do you think Jordan really cared about Timothy, or was she just trying to climb the social ladder? Explain.

3. Jordan mentions her obsessive-compulsive tendencies several times. Do you think this affected how she felt about Timothy?

4. Jordan abandoned her best friend, Kara Hendricks, in *Dark Blue*. What does she learn about friendship in *Deep Green*?

5. Jordan is tempted to have sex with Timothy in order to keep him. Do you think it would've worked? Why or why not?

6. Why was Jordan's life falling apart on every level? Obsession over Timothy? Bad choices? Lack of good friends?

7. How do you think Jordan's self-image changed during the course of the story? Improved? Deteriorated?

8. Why was Jordan so determined to get Timothy back?

9. What does it really mean to be "in love"?

10. What was Jordan's deepest need? What's yours?

TrueColors Book 3:
Torch Red

Coming in July 2004

The story of a young woman who's pretty sure she's the only virgin in her school—maybe even in the world.

One

My life is pathetic. *Really.* It's embarrassing, humiliating, totally Loserville. I mean, I can't even admit this to anyone—outside of my family, that is—but I actually spent this New Year's Eve babysitting. *Babysitting!* Now how lame is that? I mean, it was okay when I was thirteen or fourteen and needed to make a few extra bucks. But I am *sixteen,* for Pete's sake. Sixteen and three-quarters, to be precise, and I didn't even have a date for New Year's Eve.

And as long as it's time for true confessions, the sorry truth is that I've never even had a *real* honest-to-goodness boyfriend. Oh, there have been a couple of guys who've asked me out in the past year, and I actually "went steady" with Clark Harris back in middle school, but then we never even kissed. Now here I am, a junior in high school, soon to be seventeen, and I don't even have a boy-friend. So I ask you, what is wrong with me?

Oh, yeah, I *know* I'm not drop-dead gorgeous like Andrea Boswell (she could be a professional model) or that airhead cheerleader Kirsti Quackenbush, but I'm not exactly chopped liver either. And com-pared to some girls who date regularly, I'm really not *that* bad-looking. It helped getting my braces off last fall, and I haven't even had that many zits this year. My friend Emily Schuler says I look like Winona Ryder, and I'm thinking she may be on to something since I've got those same kind of dark brown eyes and straight brunette hair—although I'm not into shoplifting.

And I have to admit there are boys who do give me second looks and have even come on to me at times. But unfortunately they're usually the kinds of boys I wouldn't give a second glance anyway—guys like Spence Harding and Aaron Place. It's not that they're losers, exactly, but they don't really seem to be "boyfriend material" to me. Not that I have a right to be that picky. But I really don't want to go out with a guy who is, shall we say, *second rate*. I know that's totally shallow and pretty ridiculous, considering I just spent New Year's Eve babysitting, but I suppose I have higher hopes.

What gives me the right to nurture these high hopes? Well, I suppose that's the problem with being "marginally popular." You see, I kind of hang with a pretty cool bunch of kids. This is mostly due to my best friend, Emily (who is a cheerleader, although I'm not). And so I suppose I have this idea that *if* (and that's turning into a pretty big *if* these days) I ever date anyone, it should be some-one from within that same circle of friends.

Now, I know this is pretty stupid (did I mention shallow?) but it's like I'm in this trap and I don't really see any way out of it. And you know what really makes it seem totally absurd and crazy, or like

I'm on some sort of beat-myself-up trip? Well, there's this one particular guy that I've had this sort of secret crush on for years. His name is Nate Stein, but he's really an outsider. Not because he's not good-looking, because he *is*. In fact, he looks a little like Orlando Bloom—not with the blond braids as Legolas in *The Lord of the Rings*, but the way he normally looks with his brown hair and sultry eyes. The problem is that he's really into religion, or so I hear. And for whatever reason, that's just not cool with my crowd.

As a result, girls like Kirsti, or even Andrea and Emily, who actually are pretty nice, would never in a million years give a guy like Nate the time of day. But ever since he and I were in band together back in middle school, I've always thought he was kind of cool (and that was before Orlando became hot). But would I go out with Nate now that I'm in high school? Probably not. Now, really, how pathetic is that? I suppose I really am a shallow person. And I probably deserve exactly the kind of life I'm living.

It's just that I've had this brief reprieve during winter break. My dad decided to take our family on a ski trip to Colorado during Christmas, and it was so amazing to be away from all the crud and pressure at school. But now it's time to go back, and it's seriously getting me down. I get so bummed when I think about the disgusting things that are said in the girls' locker room every single day of the school year. And as if that's not bad enough, I feel ashamed about how I've turned into such a big fat liar this year. But how do I get out of it?

Oh, I know my lies were simply a means of survival, and you'd think in time it'd blow over. But it's like this thing I just can't seem to shake. I mean, it all started out innocently enough. It was early September, just shortly after school started. We were in the locker room getting dressed after fourth-period PE, and it seemed like every girl had to show off her new Victoria's Secret underwear—or Gap or whatever (although some girls actually clip off the labels, like if their moms bought their "unmentionables" at JCPenney or Wal-Mart). And, as usual, this underwear talk quickly led to other kinds of talk—okay, sex talk, to be precise.

Now when it comes to sex talk, some girls are more subtle and rely more on innuendo (meaning they act like they're saying something big, but you can never really pin them down or prosecute them based on their actual words). Andrea is an expert at this, as is Emily. But that is only since late last summer when she actually lost her virginity to her current boyfriend, Todd Barker. Before that, she didn't get involved in this kind of talk at all.

But then there are girls like Kirsti and her best friend, Thea Weller, who don't mind telling all (and I mean *every* skanky detail) to anyone who will listen. And let me tell you, it can get pretty disgusting at times.

"I just don't see what the big deal is," said Kirsti, who in my opinion has been a tramp since middle school. "It's just like kissing," then she giggled, "only using different body parts."

"Eeww!" said Emily as she threw her wet towel at Kirsti. "Too much information!" I tossed Emily an appreciative glance meant to convey, "Thanks for voicing my opinion exactly," as I shimmied into my jeans and quickly buttoned them before anyone noticed that I wasn't wearing a thong that day. (I happen to think they're uncomfortable.)

"Don't be such a prude," said Kirsti as she threw the towel back at Emily. *"Everyone* does it."

"Everyone does *not*," said Andrea as she adjusted what had to be the coolest bra in the locker room that day. Obviously Victoria's Secret and, I suspect, slightly padded, maybe with gel or water or whatever it is they put in those things. Thankfully, I don't need *that* kind of help.

Thea rolled her eyes at Andrea. "Well, *everyone* knows you're too much of a goody-good girl to have any real fun when it comes to guys. Lucky for you that Jamie doesn't seem to mind."

"Yeah," said Kirsti, "but you'd better watch out, Andrea, or some other babe might come along and give your boy toy a run for his money." Then she made a loud slurping noise and laughed.

"You're disgusting," said Emily as she pulled on her T-shirt.

Kirsti laughed. "Poor Emily," she said with mocking sarcasm. "We shouldn't be so shocking when there are *virgins* around."

Well, all eyes were on Emily just then. Okay, maybe some were on me too. But I got seriously nervous as I realized that *Emily was no longer a virgin*—which meant I would be the only virgin left in this big-mouthed circle of so-called friends. I think I actually began to sweat just then. Fortunately, my deodorant was nearby and I pretended to be completely absorbed in applying layer upon layer to my damp armpits. I did this with such focused perfection that I might've been auditioning for a Secret antiperspirant ad.

"You don't know *everything* about me, Kirsti," said Emily in a slightly taunting voice. "Unlike some people, I don't go around blabbering about the private details of my sex life to the entire student body."

"*Yeah.*" I could hear the disbelief in Kirsti's voice. "And we all know *why* you don't."

I glanced over my shoulder at Emily, hoping and maybe even praying that she wouldn't spill the beans. But it was too late.

"Fine," said Emily. "If you *must* know, I'm *not* a virgin anymore. There." She glanced around. "Are you happy now?"

Thea put her arm around Emily's shoulders and smiled, and I

could tell by her expression that she already knew about Emily's little secret. Still, it was weird the way Thea looked sort of like this proud mother, like Emily had just learned to ride a bike. Or maybe it was like they were in some special club together, with a secret handshake and everything. And then there was Emily, just smiling like she'd received a national honor or college scholarship or maybe even the Nobel Peace Prize. I just stared at them in amazement.

"Emily has officially joined the ranks of womanhood," Thea announced to everyone within earshot in the locker room. Several girls clapped and cheered.

"No way," said Kirsti.

"Way." Emily firmly nodded.

Kirsti frowned at Thea now. "How come you never told me?"

Thea put a finger to her lips and then winked at Emily. "Sworn to silence."

"I still don't believe it." Kirsti's eyes narrowed as she turned back to Emily.

"Whatever." Emily just shrugged like Kirsti's opinion was no big deal.

"You and Todd really did it?" asked Andrea.

"Well, it wasn't me and Zoë," said Emily as she laughed and nodded in my direction. *Thanks a lot,* I was thinking. I mean, not only did that stupid comment make me look totally lame, it was a reminder to the other girls that I was still there and, worse than that, *still* a virgin. But worst of all, I was now the *only* virgin in our group—perhaps the *only* virgin in our entire school, maybe even the planet. As I tugged on my sock, I vaguely wondered if there might be some tribe out on a deserted island somewhere who might pay good money for a real honest-to-goodness virgin—perhaps I could be used as a sacrifice somewhere to appease a volcano god or something.

I wasn't really paying too much attention to my friends' conversation after Emily's little announcement. Oh, I knew they were all congratulating Emily on her recent accomplishment. Like she'd done something really great. Yeah, right.

"So it's just Zoë now," said Thea in what actually sounded like a sympathetic voice. "The only one left." She patted me on my head as I tied my shoe. "Our little girl."

Well, *that* just got me. And it was then and there I decided that the only way out of this thing was to lie—simply and believably. And so I did.

I looked right up at Thea and, using my best poker face, told a whopper. "What makes you think *that?*"

"Huh?" Now Andrea turned around and looked at me with wide eyes. "Really? You too?"

Our area of the locker room got a lot quieter and I felt my friends all staring at me now. Without even blinking, I returned their looks (although I avoided Emily completely). I mean, if anyone could blow my cover, it would be my best friend. Just the same, I decided to risk it. I nodded at Andrea and then shrugged as if it were nothing. "Yeah, it's no big deal."

"No way," said Kirsti as she sat down on the bench beside me. "You're making this up, Zoë."

I rolled my eyes at her. "Yeah, like I would make this up."

"When?" demanded Thea. "With who?"

"Last summer," I lied like an expert. "Remember when I went to California to visit my grandma?"

"No way," said Kirsti again. "You met a guy in California?"

I smiled and nodded. "Yeah. A surfer."

"No way!" shrieked Kirsti. "You did it with a surfer dude?"

"I don't believe you," said Thea. "What's his name?"

"Daniel Englewood," I said without even blinking an eyelash. It was actually the name of a little neighbor boy that I'd babysat a couple of times while staying at my grandma's house, which, by the way, wasn't even close to a beach. "He was tan and blond and really buff." Then I actually sighed as if the memory was making me light-headed. "Daniel was so incredibly cool. I really miss him."

"Way to go," said Kirsti, patting me on the back.

"Yeah," agreed Thea, apparently convinced. "Was he good? Did you do it on the beach?"

"Oh, yeah," I said, standing up and looking at everyone, except Emily, who I knew could see right through me. "But it was more than just the sex, you know. He was really nice too. We were together the whole time I was in California. We promised to write."

"Do you love him?" asked Andrea.

I pretended to consider this. "I'm not sure," I finally said. "But he was a cool guy—a great first, you know."

It wasn't until Emily was giving me a ride home later that she questioned my little story. "You never told me about this Daniel guy, Zoë," she said as she drove away from school.

I just shrugged and looked out the window. "Everyone has some secrets."

"But I'm your best friend," she reminded me. "I told you all about Todd, practically the next day."

"Well, that was different," I told her. "You and Todd had been going together a long time. I guess I was a little embarrassed about my fling with Daniel, since I'd just met him, you know, and he lives so far away."

Emily didn't say much after that, but I sensed that I'd hurt her feelings. I even considered telling her the truth, but somehow I couldn't make myself do it. And so for the next few months, I engaged in the locker-room talk a bit more—just so I could be believable. Oh, I never actually said anything too specific when it came to sex. I followed Andrea and Emily's leads by remaining slightly aloof. But I'd sometimes laugh at Kirsti's off-color jokes and then I'd just roll my eyes at Thea's creepy descriptions of her latest sexual exploits, but all the time I just kept thinking that I didn't fit in, that I would never fit in.

And now that it's time to go back to school again, it seems more painfully obvious than ever that (1) I don't even have a boyfriend, (2) I am living a complete lie, and (3) I am the last virgin remaining on the planet.

about the author

MELODY CARLSON has written dozens of books for all age groups, but she particularly enjoys writing for teens. Perhaps this is because her own teen years remain so vivid in her memory. After claiming to be an atheist at the ripe old age of twelve, she later surrendered her heart to Jesus and has been following him ever since. Her hope and prayer for all her readers is that each one would be touched by God in a special way through her stories. For more information, please visit Melody's website at www.melodycarlson.com.

Lonely? Jealous? Hurt?
Melody Carlson addresses the issues you face today.

The TrueColors Series

The TrueColors series addresses issues that most affect teen girls. By taking on these difficult topics without being phony or preachy, best-selling author Melody Carlson challenges you to stay true to who you are and what you believe.

Dark Blue
(Loneliness)
9781576835296

Deep Green
(Jealousy)
9781576835302

Torch Red
(Sex)
9781576835319

Pitch Black
(Suicide)
9781576835326

Burnt Orange
(Drinking)
9781576835333

Fool's Gold
(Materialism)
9781576835340

Blade Silver
(Cutting)
9781576835357

Bitter Rose
(Divorce)
9781576835364

Faded Denim
(Eating Disorders)
9781576835371

Bright Purple
(Homosexuality)
9781576839508

Moon White
(Witchcraft)
9781576839515

Harsh Pink
(Popularity)
9781576839522

9781576835296

9781576835319

9781576835302

9781576835364

To order copies, call NavPress at
1-800-366-7788 or log on to
www.NavPress.com.

TH1NK *by* NavPress